Maggie Donner's Dating Quiz

1. If you're looking for a man, you should

(a) join a dating service

(b) invest in a leather skirt

(c) collide with a hunk's truck during a blizzard

2. When meeting a man for the first time, always

(a) smile prettily and bat your eyelashes

(b) offer him your hand and say, "How do you do?"

(c) apologize for your attempted homicide

3. Proper dating etiquette for the nineties recommends you:

(a) never gamble with stakes higher than a two-dollar watch

(b) always order the roast meat at a truck stop

(c) determine a man's marital status before you spend the night in his truck on the side of a highway

4. When you find a man like Ruffan Reddy:

(a) don't let him go until you get his license number

(b) don't let him go until you get his phone number

(c) don't let him go!

Dear Reader,

Picture this: you're a single woman and you still haven't met Mr. Right. You're not even fretting about this as you drive along the highway, when suddenly, *boom!* A fender bender. You're steaming mad—until you notice the other driver is tall, dark and *very* apologetic as he hands over his name and address in the form of his license and registration.

Of course I'm not suggesting you should try this at home. But it sure works for Maggie Donner in Lass Small's *Not Looking for a Texas Man.* (Especially once they're stuck together in his truck, waiting for help—*overnight.*)

An easier way to meet the man of your dreams is to buy him. And that's exactly what Noelle Perry does in Tiffany White's *Male for Sale.* Imagine: you're dateless for your *younger* sister's wedding, so you secretly buy a hunk at a bachelor auction—and hope he'll exchange his black leather jacket for a tuxedo. I know, money can't buy love—but maybe it can buy Noelle a date for the next three thousand Saturday nights.

Next month, look for two new entertaining, engaging Yours Truly novels by Cait London and Toni Collins— with two more unexpected ways to meet, date…and marry Mr. Right!

Yours truly,

Melissa Senate

Editor

Please address questions and book requests to:
Silhouette Reader Service
U.S.: 3010 Walden Ave., P.O. Box 1325, Buffalo, NY 14269
Canadian: P.O. Box 609, Fort Erie, Ont. L2A 5X3

LASS SMALL

Not Looking for a Texas Man

SILHOUETTE YOURS TRULY™

Published by Silhouette Books

America's Publisher of Contemporary Romance

SILHOUETTE BOOKS

ISBN 0-373-52004-2

NOT LOOKING FOR A TEXAS MAN

Copyright © 1995 by Lass Small

Printed in U.S.A.

About the author

"In 1993, I received a remarkable, gently flattering letter saying I was chosen as one of thirty-seven STARS for Fort Wayne's 1994 Bicentennial. However, the letter was addressed to *Mr.* Lass *Smith.* I told one of the letter's signers that I was female, my last name was Small and the letter was so marvelous that Mr. Smith should have the copy. The woman said, 'No, no. It's you we want. Just mark the name out and change it.' Hilarious. 1994's October STAR gala was elegant, and this TEXAS woman now has a Yankee Bicentennial medallion that is precious.

"There have been other salutes. Harlequin-Silhouette gave me an Award of Excellence for *Contact.* It was my twenty-fifth published book. Bookstores That Care, *Romantic Times* and Romance Writers of America have given me awards and trophies. Then there are the reader letters, which touch my heart and on occasion make my eyes tear even as I smile.

"Not Looking for a Texas Man is being published in September, which is my birth month. Not counting reissues, this is *my fiftieth published book!*

"Salute to it, the new Yours Truly line and all readers."

With my love,
Lass Small

To my son-in-law, Roger Johnson, who is curious
about all the world and who has investigated
many things, including trucks, tractor cabs and
driving the things

1

━━▶ ◀━━

That February, in Indiana's long-term weather forecast, there had been a mention of possibly severe cold. Now, how many times lately had that come true? They warn and indicate on a projected map and talk about it, but they do emphasize it is only a possibility.

While anyone knows it's going to be cold in winter, up there, the really bad storm generally doesn't happen. When it does, they're all surprised.

So Maggie Donner, being all of twenty-six, wasn't convinced by the national TV weatherman on her motel screen. Even though she was a stranger in the area, she checked only the national news.

Maggie was a good looker. Well, she did look good, but she also was an excellent scanner of territory. She matched up terrain with script location sites for films.

At that time in the beginning of the year, the snowfall in Indiana was unusual. It had been twenty years since there had been such a winter. The production staff, for which Maggie worked, eagerly wanted a nice, midwestern, rural, Christmas-card snow.

So, on cue, it had snowed. Of course. The film crew had needed it, and so it was!

The only problem with that year's snow was the really serious cold. And Maggie was from TEXAS. Sending her out into that weather mass was like pitching a chick out of the incubator too soon.

She was what her grandfather called a "chick." The term dated him considerably. She was slender, long-legged, nicely rounded—here and there—with a thick mane of red-brown hair. Her eyes were green.

The night before, she had set her little digital timer and slept. When the dinger suggested it was time, she got up. She pulled on the TEXAS version of long underwear and a flamboyantly green workout suit with a flannel-lined jacket. She wore short ankle boots and even had earmuffs. But she wore those mainly because the band kept her hair back.

Maggie took her bag and went out to her car. She drove around to the front of the motel and parked under the overhang like those on every motel she'd seen. She noted the car's gas tank was indeed full; therefore, the oil had been checked. The tires were new. Her daddy had seen to that.

In the car, she had water and granola bars inside a thick old army comforter her grandfather had had in WWII. The reason she had it was that, in the South Pacific, he'd never needed it. That excess had all been put in Maggie's car by her mother. And Maggie was therefore more than ready to join the hurrying vehicles which roared through the snow on past the motel.

What . . . vehicles?

Well, it was early yet. She'd risen to get an early start. Her watch said it was nine already. In winter, that was early enough.

She didn't look like she was a native from anywhere the desk clerk could remember. He said, "We've got some cold weather out there."

Maggie smiled and brushed her hair back to show her earmuffs. That proved she was over sixteen after all and ready for cold weather. She even said, "I'm ready for it."

She paid her bill. And the clerk watched her seriously. He said, "You be careful. It's cold."

Of course, TEXAS "cold" and Yankee "cold" are two different things. So a confident Maggie replied, "I can handle it." She gave him a slight smile that generally knocked men clean off their feet. The desk clerk was older and securely married so he only blinked.

Maggie gathered her card and receipt to stride from his presence, out through the doors and back to her trusty little white car.

He had her TEXAS license number. The TEXAS state outline was dark blue and showed up nicely on the white background. He had her name. He frowned after her. She was about his middle daughter's age.

Maggie drove from the access road onto highway I-69 and was pleased it wasn't crowded. She didn't turn on a news station. She put in a tape, punched the buttons and sat back for the smooth ride to Indy.

Quite soon, she realized the car's heater wasn't working properly. The road was slippery. The wind was swirling the snow, making seeing difficult. There were cars pulled off to the side. Maggie slowed and stretched to see but apparently the cars were empty. There were even *trucks* off on the sides of the double highway.

There was no way she could push a truck with her little white car. But the trucks were silent and the lights were off.

It was bitterly cold. She felt the vents for warm air, and the flow was feeble. There must be something she could do about the heat. She slowed and . . .

All the trucker could see was the dark blue state of TEXAS license plate.

The trucker blew his horn like a freight train.

She looked up because she was already on the outside lane. How much room did he— She couldn't see out of the snow-covered back window. She looked at the side-view mirror on the door. The truck was sliding sideways and coming right at her!

She tried to floor the gas pedal and it only made her car swerve and skid. She was going to be hit! She could die right there!

With Herculean effort, the truck driver turned his cab so that his front bumper hit her car, knocked most of the snow off and pushed her faster than she'd been going. She had no control. They went off into the snow on the side of the road at the next slight curve. Her car was pushed on, down the slope out of sight, but it was not under the truck. It was ahead of it.

She was all right. Her car would need help getting out of there. She got her seat belt unbuckled. Her car door was jammed. The truck covered the entire back window. She couldn't get out. She didn't know if the truck driver was all right or if—together—they were going to explode into a gigantic fireball.

Well, she worked with people who used their imaginations.

She was aware the winds were blowing. The cold, cold snow was lifted and it was like a ground blizzard. Maggie began to be tolerant of her mother's including the blanket.

A great big, enormous man loomed like a genie right beside her and, even knowing someone had to be in that great semi, his presence surprised her.

Her window was frosted. The whole inside of her car was a blank. With her breath and the still-running heater... She turned off the car key.

He took hold of her door handle, put his foot on the side of her car and he jerked the door open. Good gravy! Think of the power men have!

She looked up at a carefully wrapped mummy. She instantly realized the mummy had escaped from Chicago's Field Museum. He was out, free at last. He was going to give her a strange potion, mummify her and take her back to his casket.

She asked, "Are you all right?"

He replied with great control, "A white car on snow is not noticeable. Pitch this o— When we get you a new car, please ask for red."

"Why would you get me a new car? I have insurance. I'm covered." She was shivering with the door open, but she was being polite.

He growled. "This one's finished. Come on. The tractor cab's warmer. Where's your coat?"

She was somewhat indignant over his ignorance. The fingers of her left hand picked at her jacket to indicate she was suitably covered.

He put his head down into the door, and she drew back, somewhat startled. There was no way, at all, that he could get into her car, too.

He reached over into the back seat and hauled out the WWII blanket. He caught the thermos and rolled it in the blanket. He said, "I'll come back for you."

He closed the door enough and just...left her there. He'd snatched her blanket and water. She looked into the back seat. The granola box was on the floor. She got her camera and the granola package and stacked them with her shoulder sling purse as he came back.

He opened the door and held out a big shaggy sheepskin coat for her. "Get into this."

Since she was shivering—from nerves caused by the circumstances—she slid out of the car and was instantly wrapped in a static, warm covering. It had been in his truck. It was heavenly. She closed her eyes and admitted she'd been quite chilled.

Maggie was of the ilk who didn't see danger in mice or anything distasteful. As long as she didn't acknowledge anything like that, it didn't exist. In that instance, she had not yet admitted to being cold.

He said, "Go get in the cab. Bring your keys."

Maggie considered disobeying such blunt directions. He hadn't asked if she'd mind or if she would. He'd told her to go get in the truck and bring her keys.

And she considered that he'd taken her thermos with the thick WWII blanket.

She looked around. She decided on her own that the truck would be better than where she was. She got her camera bag, the keys, her purse, her overnight bag and the granola bars.

As she got out of the car, she was surprised to find the snow was so deep. Her boots were ankle high. Up until then, that had been sufficient. They were no longer.

She looked at the rear end of her car. It was vulgarly crumpled, much like a sheet of paper. She didn't say anything. She was his guest and guests don't speak of controversial things to one's host. One goes through a lawyer.

She was taking her first steps when he bent down and quite effortlessly picked her up and carried her over to his truck cab. He braced one foot on his opposite knee to hold her and his freed hand swept the blowing snow off the steps.

He put her feet on the first step and braced his hand on her back to hold her steady as he opened the door. He said, "Get inside."

And she did.

She crawled across the middle seat gap to the passenger side as he climbed up and closed the door. It was marvelously, deliciously warm inside. She shivered. She was frozen. She finally admitted to herself that he'd probably saved her life by ramming her car.

He put her blanket in the space between the seats where the gears were. He undid his face coverings and slid out of his jacket. He punched a button and said into a piece that was a communications system, "This is Rabbit. Any hounds around?"

She thought, What have I gotten into?

A reply came, "This here's Red Dog. What's the problem?"

"I've gone off the road, taking a little white car with me. Nobody's hurt." He gave the marker number and distance and what all.

She knew truckers had communication abilities, but she'd never known they had such a network. It was fascinating.

Other truckers along the way called in saying where they were and who needed help and one truck had three tourists inside with him. Any nontrucker was a tourist.

She was still shivering.

As he gave her license number, he looked over at her from under his bushy eyebrows and through his thick lashes and asked, "What's your name? This is to report to the state cops. Got your insurance card?"

She replied. "I was going at a moderate speed because of the condition of the highway."

He replied patiently, "It was entirely my fault. We need your name because your momma will be getting panicky and somebody needs to know you're okay, here with me."

By then she had looked at him and her breathing became sporadic and her heartbeat was odd. She wasn't attracted to him. He was a coarse, unmannerly person. Such a one had no lure to her. She replied, "I'm Margaret Donner, en route to Indianapolis."

He looked at her for just a minute, then he reported her name and destination.

When he broke off communication, she said, "Since you know my name, what is yours?"

"I'm Ruffan Reddy." Then he looked at her tolerantly and spelled it.

She nodded in tiny, tight-lipped bobs. Everyone knows about truck drivers. The Knights of the Road. Their chatter can be cleverly rough. She could tolerate someone called, for Pete's sake, Ruffan... Reddy? Rough and ready. How juvenile.

She tilted her head formally and said, "How do you do?"

"Better." He smiled, his eyelashes screening his eyes.

What did he mean by that?

He asked, "Would you like a drink of water?"

"I believe you have my thermos?"

"It's frozen."

She was startled. "How could it freeze? It was wrapped in the blanket."

"It's been very cold. You probably left it in the car last night."

"How can you know that?"

"You have a Texas license plate. What're you doing in Indiana?"

"I'm... visiting."

"Do you want to call anybody? I can arrange it." He indicated the speaker to the CB.

"Not yet." She watched him in eye flicks so as not to appear to stare. "I can't believe my thermos is frozen."

He reached under his seat and brought out her thermos. "You need to give it more time to thaw. Do you only drink Texas water?"

She tilted her nose up a notch and reminded him, "TEXAS is always said and written in capitals?" It was the do-you-understand questioning statement. "That's twice you've pretended TEXAS is just like any other state."

"I hadn't realized it. You're my first."

Hesitantly she asked, "First . . . what? Rescue?"

"Naw. We find people in the damnedest places. People are mostly weird. You're my first TEXAN. There, was that right?"

She was prissy. "A shade more vocal respect."

He laughed.

She inquired, "Do you smoke?"

"Naw. You'll have to step outside if you exhale."

"I don't smoke. I was worried you did."

"In this weather, being inside with smokers beats being outside with pure air."

"I do believe you could be correct."

"You don't talk like any Tex—TEXAN I've ever heard."

"I went to a very strict school and I have a mother who was an English Teacher. Those first two letters are capitalized."

"I had one of those. She threw up—no, it was just her hands—over me."

And Maggie laughed as she began to relax. She said, "This coat is simply marvelous. How can you lend it to me? You might never get it back as long as I'm above the Mason-Dixon line."

"I'm insulated."

She looked at him. "You're not fat."

"I'm a Yankee."

"Baseball?"

"Native. I'm a Northerner. We adjust to the weather. Most of us prefer the winter."

"Daddy has always said that Northerners were strange. I believe his actual word was 'different.' As children, we were curious about the dam-yankees." She quickly lifted one hand as she tilted her head courteously. "At home, it's always said as one word."

He sat behind the steering wheel, relaxed, with one big square hand, turned thumb outward, on his left thigh. His other big hand was spread on the other thigh. He watched her mostly but he also glanced around.

He wore a lumberjack shirt and the turtleneck of long underwear was visible at his throat. His hair was a little shaggy, like his eyebrows. He was a really beautiful male. Geo would be interested in him for the film.

She asked, "Would you be interested in allowing a filmed audition?"

He regarded her. "What for?"

"Some people look great but don't photograph well. You might. If you would be interested, where could I have a crew contact you?"

"Not me."

She was surprised. Wasn't Clark Gable a truck driver when he was found? "Why not?"

"I'm just not interested in something like that. Is that what you do? Are you a scout?"

"No. I'm nobody." He didn't protest that. She then elaborated. "I look for sites for photo background." That was the bare bones.

"What sort're you looking for?"

"Farms."

"There's some real bucolic ones just off this highway. Over that way. You might be interested. Little towns, church spires. Stuff like that."

They watched as a big semi went creeping carefully along. The radio asked, "You need any help?"

Ruff replied, "Thank you. We got help coming, but it could be a while. Be careful."

"Yep."

She said, "All those trucks and cars along the way, are they okay?"

"Those you saw are empty. I checked. There could be some added ones, but nobody's called in yet. I think those were from last night." He looked at her. "We'll replace your car, but if you're gonna run around the north in winter, be sure not to get another white one. With your car loaded with snow and ice thata way, I didn't see you until just before I hit you.

If I hadn't seen your license, I'd not have hit the brakes, and it would have been a whole lot worse."

"You really did a very polite job of it. I just slid along."

"I was really wrestling the wheel. The trailer woulda gone sideways, and you'd of been crushed under it. I really sweat and I couldn't even swear. I was so shocked that a car would be there. You're sure you're okay?"

"I'm really all right." She shook the thermos. "Do you think it's thawed?"

"Oh, hell, I forgot. Let me." He took a cup and put it under the spigot, filling the cup effortlessly. "The cup's practically clean." He wiped it with his sleeve and handed it to her.

She drank slowly, looking out at the falling snow. Her eyes found a thermometer. It read twenty below zero. "Twenty... below?"

"Yeah. That's not counting windchill. What are you doing out on a highway on a day like today?"

She considered. "Exploring new acquaintances?"

And that's when she caught his full attention. She'd already had his male awareness. But she had never once complained or whined or fretted.

Nothing else came past them. It was as if they were alone in the whole universe. She said, "I have a younger brother who is a little strange. He made audio tapes of adventures. In one, he was the last living person on the planet. He was inside a capsuled communication station. The whole world was ruined by a terrible war. And he told of it into a recorder. He ended it asking, 'Is anybody out there?' And there was no reply. The tape ran on with only small air sounds. It was very... poignant.''

Ruff nodded. "Guys go through that stage. He was probably one of the first computer geniuses."

"He is."

"Just you two?"

"No. Another brother and two sisters. My parents are so embarrassed. They really intended having only the allotted two, but they were surprised three times. Mother said we extras were a shock, and warned us that there's no such thing as a 'safe period.' ''

He was a little surprised she'd actually said that. But he smiled almost and replied, "My parents just have me. They wanted a girl. They always look at me in some surprise that I'm not. Mother is particularly disgruntled."

She said with a laugh, "Here we are, strangers, and we are discussing our parents in a quite intimate manner. I have heard this happens when people are isolated briefly. They speak of things they would ordinarily never share with a friend. Do you have anything you'd like to get off your chest?"

"I've been wondering how you'd be in bed."

She became instantly stilled without moving a muscle. He'd shocked her. She straightened primly but that only made her chest more obvious.

He smiled a little and watched her, very amused and highly entertained.

She said, "I really didn't mean for our conversation to become personal." Her accent was a little thicker.

"I'm not going to force you. I was just answering your question."

There was a very empty pause and then she inquired, "Where did you go to school?"

And his soft laughter was unstoppable.

Sober faced and somewhat stiff, she didn't look at him, nor did she comment.

After an awkward while, the CB speaker said, "Hey, Ruff, we're having a hell of a time with this weather. We're trying to find a truck to get you out of there. You said the trailer's over on its side?"

"Not entirely. But the wheel is twisted. I need some help to get it loose from the tractor."

"Thank God it wasn't loaded. You can leave it there. Is it off the road enough?"

"Yeah."

"What about the car? Is the driver okay?"

"Yeah. She's in the cab with me."

"Give her our kindest regards and treat her like a princess so she doesn't sue us."

"She says she has her own insurance and doesn't need ours."

"Well, how'd you work that?"

"Her car is as white as the snow."

There was a brief silence. "We might be able to go with that angle." There was another silence. "We'll get help to you." There was another pause, and he said,

"We'll take good care of her." And he added, "Ruff, be cordial."

Ruff tried not to laugh out loud. He said, "That'll be the easy part."

"She's a looker?"

"She waggles a man's...eyes."

"Behave."

Ruff looked over at the nubile princess and asked, "Hear that? It was orders. You're safe. Damn."

She lifted her chin just a tad and replied, "I wasn't worried."

Under those eyelashes, he slid his look over at her. "You're lucky."

"Bushwah."

"What's that mean?"

She replied, "It's TEXAN for 'nonsense.' "

"That word's acceptable in polite society?"

She considered. "Actually, it was probably adjusted from something outrageously vulgar."

He smiled a bit. "Have you figured out what it might be?"

"I shun vulgarities. There are enough words in the language to speak clearly, in mood or anger without being snotty."

"*You* would use a crass word like—snotty?"

She replied gently, "While it is crass, it is not vulgar."

"My momma would make me lick a bar of soap over that one."

"She is a lady."

"Relentlessly."

"Most ladies are. It's their only protection. I'd bet your daddy smokes outside."

"No. She does."

That hit Maggie's funny bone and she laughed out loud.

He considered the surprise that she might be tolerable. And his eyes went again down her body. She had put off the great shaggy coat and was sitting in its curl of protection. She looked like a newly hatched miracle.

Such women were a burden, a nuisance, a nerve-straining trial. He wanted no part of her. But they would be together until help got there. His eyes might just as well entertain him, and his libido might just as well dream. Her mouth was really sweet and soft. Her body was female. Very female.

This one was like some women. If she isn't aware of herself, she's a person, not a woman. If *her* awareness isn't there, then neither is there interest from an observer. Some women are that dumb.

Maybe not dumb. Maybe they're just lacking in self-image. They honestly don't think of other people's attention to them. She sat over there now, like a cat that's licked its fur in front of the fireplace and is contented. A cat never notices people unless they open the refrigerator door.

Ruff wondered what she equated to a cat's refrigerator door? What would catch her attention?

He didn't need any woman. Out there in the middle of Indiana, he didn't need to get trapped by some nubile innocent who really didn't have the brains to stay put and not go gallivanting off down a highway in a white car in blowing snow. A dumb redhead.

But God. She was really something. He would not allow himself to get tempted. He'd be cool and distant and he'd survive this encounter.

Yeah.

Sure.

And in the years ahead, just watch, he'd dream about her and regret not having tried.

He looked at her in a weighing manner. Would she? He gave the opening, "You—"

And the CB broke in, "It'll be a while. Do you have something red to put out the window? With the wind blowing the snow, they might have trouble finding you."

He asked the luring witch who shared his cab. "You got a red scarf?"

She looked at him and pulled her head back a tad and squinted her face as if in pain as she inquired, "With *this* hair?"

He smiled. "Yeah."

"How about yellow?"

He got to watch as she moved around, turning her body and searching in her pockets. She was *fascinating* to watch.

Like a magician, she took the end of the silken scarf from inside one pocket and pulled it out in a long, brilliant streak of yellow. Only she could wear something that strong and not be overwhelmed. Interesting.

He said to the CB, "We've got yellow, and I'll turn on the lights."

"I'd've thought they were already on."

"We have the heater on. She's a TEXAS girl and she's dressed thataway."

"You're losing it, Ruff?"

"Temporarily."

"You mean—"

"You'll get a report."

She asked, "Is the CB going out?"

Ruff shook his head. "No, we are. Just as soon as help gets here."

"Where will we go?"

"Down the road ahead of us is a cutoff to a fine truck stop. There's a store and café, a filling station, a big truck parking lot and some cabins. We'll find a place."

"What'll happen to my car and your trailer?"

"It'll be a day or two until they can get them out and get them back for evaluation. The wind is strong and the snow'll pile up."

"Is there a car rental where we're going?"

"I seriously doubt it."

"I'll be stranded there?"

"I'll take care of you. Don't worry about a thing." He looked over at her and from behind his dark eyelashes, his eyes smiled.

Something shivered inside her.

2

Neither Maggie nor Ruff was a real talker. Their conversations were only comfortably sporadic. They sat listening to the wind, and both were glad not to be out of the cab.

Ruff told her, "I need to get out of some layers." He indicated his covered body. "Could I turn the heat down a little?"

She looked at him as if she'd just met the Abominable Snowman. "You're too...warm?"

"I'm sweating."

"How could you poss— Men are strange." She began to put her arms back into the shaggy coat.

That appalled him. "No! I'll just peel down a little. Don't get panicked. Truck drivers dress in layers. I can go down a couple." He couldn't stand to have her more covered than she already was, therefore he'd have to peel down.

With real curiosity Maggie asked, "How did you get in the truck business?"

"It beats sitting behind a desk or sorting mail."

She could understand that. "You must meet interesting people."

"And some that are nasty."

She nodded to confirm her considering agreement. "People are different in varying manners. I have a friend in the U.S. Attorney's office down in TEXAS? She says the agents are so hardened by their jobs dealing with people who are so rough that the agents become another race of men entirely. Are truck drivers like that?"

"We're all gentle travelers who enjoy the scenery and help people in distress. I'll bet you've never changed your own tire."

"I have the kind that will stay inflated long enough to get the car to the next town."

He nodded. "Smart." Then he recognized he had an opening and glanced over at her as he asked, "Your husband tell you to do that?"

She corrected gently, "The brother who is the computer genius. The others in the family don't understand the premise of isolation?" It was the questioning, do-you-understand statement.

But he pushed it. "You have a husband?"

"No." She looked up at him in some surprise. "Why do you ask?"

Slick as could be, he replied, "I needed to know if he might be worried about you." He indicated the CB.

"Oh."

"I'm not married, either."

She looked at him again. She tilted her head back a little, which increased her narrow-eyed look of disbelief. "Recently divorced?"

"Never married." He smiled his innocent smile. It was his healthy, young man in a close encounter, maybe, situation.

"I deduce that you are rarely in a situation that you're forced to be idle."

He nodded in a positive up and down as he admitted, "I am a man of action." He licked his lips and his smile was a tad larger.

She moved that body around as she found her purse and zipped it open in a busy way.

He shivered in anticipation. A condom?

She took out two decks of cards.

He couldn't believe it. He sat, immobilized and silent.

She handed him one deck. "While they are shuffled, you may reshuffle. We are going to play War."

"War?"

"Along the way, I visited my older sister? In north TEXAS? She has two kids who are restless. When I walked in the front door, she went right out the back door yelling, 'I'll be back.' There I was—alone—with the two monsters. We went shopping. I tied ropes on them. People stared. However, the two did not get away. I bought cards. We went back to their house and played War. I'm very competitive. They share that gene."

He considered her. She could handle anything. Look how she'd been all this time. Never once had she seemed hesitant or reluctant or uncomfortable. She'd never gushed or flirted or worried. She'd accepted the whole situation with great adjustment. Two recalcitrant kids wouldn't faze her. Her solution had been just right.

Even for him.

With his eyelashes almost together, he asked, "What are we betting?"

She looked at him in brief surprise. Then she opened her purse wider and pulled out a plastic, two-dollar Burger King watch. She laid it on her grand-daddy's WWII blanket, which filled the gap between their seats.

He tucked his lower lip under his upper teeth before he inquired kindly, "Are you sure you want to risk that in a game of chance?"

Just his word choice made the gong sound. Her mother had told Maggie she'd hear a mental gong if she was in danger. Her mother had said, "If you ever get into a sly situation, you'll be aware of it because you'll hear the gong sound. That's a communication from your guardian. When you hear a gong, get out of there."

Her mother had been right.

So Maggie glanced around at the strongly blowing snow screen covering the windshield and the eastside window and enclosing Margaret Donner in a dangerous capsule. She was isolated with a potently interesting man. And she wondered just what sort of getaway her mother would recommend in this particular situation?

Maggie would see.

She replied. "I have three of these watches? I also bought the kids each one when I took them to lunch.

There are just days when one does not care to eat or see another peanut-butter sandwich?'' She was inquiring if he understood what she was saying.

He nodded.

''I bought three of the watches and the betting did limit how many games of War we would play. We went outside after that, and I showed them how to teach their dog to obey.''

''You terrify me.'' But he lied. He smiled and his eyes sparkled behind that barrier of lashes.

When a woman realizes the man can lie, it solves believing him.

He asked, ''Is this a Strip Poker War?''

''The rule is, when you win all my watches, we quit.''

''You're not as competitive as you claimed.''

She agreed, ''Only somewhat. I am also practical.''

''I bet those little kids cried when you left.''

''Actually, they did. My sister came home, and they didn't want to let her inside. I was teaching them how to stop the dog from barking. It was the ideal time for the dog to learn. They didn't want to be distracted. I asked Nell to sit on the porch swing for fifteen minutes. She did. We let her in later.''

Ruff watched Maggie for a while. ''How long will your lessons stay with them?''

''They are kin. They're idle and bored. It will be a challenge for them and they'll persevere.''

''Why hadn't your sister taught them those ways?''

''She's distracted by her company. My brother-in-law is a lawyer and my sister owns several filling stations. The kids know everything there is to know about a car. I let them change my oil. They got everything just right."

"How...old...are they?"

"He's six. She is eight." She waited for a minute. Then she smiled a little before she told him, "When I left, I went to a service station and asked them to check the oil out. The kids had done it perfectly. I can't change oil."

"You sound like a genius."

"I have some gifts in some things. I play a mean game of cards. What are you putting up against my two-dollar watch? No money. As children, we were forbidden to risk money. The habit sticks."

He looked for anything he might use as a nonmoney bet. It finally came to a Joe Montana baseball cap the quarterback had worn after a football game. It was autographed. Ruff smiled as he put it on. He requested she change decks with him.

They played War.

They were so animated by the game that they had to turn the heater down. They leaned forward and they competed! It really was *war!* But they learned a lot about each other. They also laughed, they argued with waving hands and they were funny.

They leaned back and grinned at each other. They played again. Cards, that is. And her Burger King watch went back and forth. But only that. Joe's baseball cap was never in jeopardy.

As was inevitable, she eventually had to find a way to relieve herself. She said, "With the wind blowing against your side, I should be able to slip out this side for a minute?''

He demurred, ''This is a cross-country capsule, we have everything but a cooking stove. We have a bed. We even have a sink back there. But we also have a urinal. It's in back. We have women drivers so the top's been adjusted. You'll have only to take out the plug. It screws.'' He looked at her soberly. Actually, he owned several of the trucks.

''I'll just go outside.''

''Honey, your bottom would freeze. Use the other way. I'll step out and check our visibility. We don't want our rescuers passing us by.''

So she went over into the back of the cab and looked around in delight. A neat, tidy bed, a lavatory and sure enough, there was an adjusted urinal! All the comforts of home!

When he came back inside, he came in her door. He was wearing the shaggy coat and shook off the blowing snow as she shifted to let him move back under the wheel.

He'd scraped off the windshield, the side windows and the lights. With the trailer leaned over only enough to bend the connecting wheel, the printing on the side had been covered by the blowing snow.

With the pure cold air still surrounding him, Ruff settled in behind the wheel and called in on the CB. ''We're getting a strong ground wind from the east so the snow has covered the side of the trailer. Whoever is coming for us will have to keep in touch so he doesn't pass us.''

The speaker replied, "When we find somebody loose, he'll find you."

"I'm not sure he'll be able to see the mile markers."

"We'll find you. You have food?"

"Yeah."

"We'll be there as soon as we can. There're a lot of trucks off. Some injuries."

"Who?" Ruff asked.

"None of ours."

Ruff promised, "We're okay. Don't worry about us. We have food and water. We'll be okay as long as the cab's heated. We have enough gas for forty-two hours. Even then, we're inside and we have water, food and blankets." Then Ruff enunciated carefully, "We also have two decks of cards."

Whoever was listening laughed before the contact said, "We'll let you know when we're coming."

Lunch was interesting. The sandwiches he shared were made with thick bread and piled between the slices were ham, cheese, tomatoes, lettuce and onions. Red onions.

Maggie managed a third of one and was stuffed. He ate all of his and the rest of hers. They had both been for him. For dessert, she gave him a caramel from her purse. He was grateful.

In that long time, there had been a couple of occasional trucks, which had crept on by them, very slowly, the drivers asking, "You okay?"

Ruff replied, "Be careful. We're reported in. We're on the rescue list."

"That Ruff?"

"Yeah."

"Now how in the *world* did you git there?"

"I ran over a white car."

"That's plausible. Anybody hurt?"

"No. I saw her in time."

That "her" was a slip. Now, everybody listening knew there was a woman in his cab with him. "She's a lady who had been in this world for some time."

He'd made it seem as if Maggie was old.

"She okay?"

"Yeah. We're playing two-handed bridge."

That made for a lot of laughs. Poor old Ruffan Reddy was trapped in a wind-driven snowstorm with an old lady and playing bridge!

Maggie had understood the exchange. She wondered why he made it appear the way he had. Almost instantly, she understood. He was protecting her. And himself. There were pirates along the road. Some still mobile trucker could "rescue" her?

Naw. Not in this day and age. Then she remembered her daddy had warned her about all the women who had died in Indiana in the past ten years who'd been killed by truckers. Most had been hookers working truck stops.

But some of the women had been en route to college, and some had never been found. They'd last been seen with their car's hood up talking to a trucker. That was the last time they were seen alive. Long afterward, two were found by farmers in their fields.

So why did Maggie feel she was safe with a man named Ruffan Reddy?

Well.

Because he had reported her presence to someone else. Most of his listeners believed she was elderly and they were spending their trapped time playing bridge. He hadn't allowed anyone to think of him as being with a young woman, that they were alone together in a disabled truck or that she could be vulnerable.

She looked over at Ruff, and he was aware of her movement. He glanced back. Their gazes locked as she considered him. Then she smiled just a tad.

He said, "Do you want a nap? You can have the bed in back."

There were limits to any age woman. She said, "No, thank you."

"If you don't want that bed, I think I'll take a cat-nap. This has been one hell of a day."

Quite openly, she replied, "And I am responsible. My insurance should cover it all."

He looked at her in what she considered blank endurance. But he told her, "If I'd been paying more attention, I wouldn't have overrode you. It was my fault."

"If you declare that, I believe my insurance company will clap their little hands and breathe rapidly in their delight."

Ruff smiled slightly and said, "Mine won't. They'll be grouchy and their breaths will be hot with temper."

"But they'll be courteous."

"Stringently."

She inquired, "Do you have tattoos?"

"I wasn't Navy."

"Not a pirate?"

"Not in this life." He grinned.

So he admitted he'd probably been one in another life? His big truck was a landlocked ship of another sort.

With lithe movements, he pulled himself up and over the back of the seat onto the bed behind them. He said, "Don't try to escape."

She chuffed in rejection of such a thing being plausible.

Another truck eased on past them. They said on the radio, "You okay in there?"

Maggie asked, "How do I reply?"

Ruff leaned over, bracing a hand on the seat as he replied, "No problem."

"You got a woman in there?"

Ruff leaned forward again and said, "She's the driver." Then he lowered his voice to a harsh whisper. "She's even built like a truck driver."

"We heard she was a little old lady."

"She's not that fragile," Ruff was saying. "She's got arms like a stevedore. I'd bet she could arm wrestle you."

"You scare me."

In a whisper, Ruff complained, "Think of sharing the cab with her."

"How can you talk like that in front of a lady?"

"She's in the back, sleeping. I had to turn her over. She snores like my grandpaw."

Maggie's eyes sparkled and her hands covered her mouth to smother her laughter.

He turned off the speaker and sighed. "We're going to get questions as long as the trucks manage to pass us. You might as well get in back and read, and I'll sleep along the seat. Okay?"

She replied cheerfully, "Your house—your rules." She gathered her things and therefore didn't see his expression.

A flicker went through him. His rules? Well, okay! Yeah. Sure. He put a pillow onto the front seat and slid his stocking feet down to the seat.

Her blanket was still between the seats, making it comfortable to lie across them. He asked, "Will you need the sheepskin coat?"

"No. I have my jacket."

"That's a blouse." He was disparaging. "You don't have anything near a coat. Can you snuggle down in the blankets or do you need the coat, too?"

"I'll be warm."

"If you get cold, get under the mattress pad, too. Or you can come over into the front, and I'll g-give you the coat and turn up the cab's heat."

"Put the coat between the seats and use my blanket for cover."

"I'd forgotten you came prepared. My granddaddy had one of these. They're really warm. With the blankets back there, you'll be fine. I'll use your blanket."

Then quickly he said, "Uh, let me see what you'll have handy to read. He went back into the bed area and began to go quickly through the magazines. He couldn't find anything she should read. He frowned at her. "This 'library' wasn't assembled for nubile females."

She said, "I can manage. I've read *Playboy* magazines."

"Uh, these are just a little further along that idea."

"I can handle it. Some of the best articles I've read were from *Playboy*. One short story was about a loused-up bank robbery. They tunneled in as the bank was robbed from the street, and the customers who were forced into the vault thought the tunnelers were the FBI."

"I read that."

She laughed.

"Now." He squinted at her. "Why did you laugh because I said I'd read it?"

"You were being so pure."

"I didn't say I looked at the nekkid women!"

"How noble of you."

"Well, I have peeked..." He glanced at her hair. "At the redheads to see if they were real redheads."

"There's all kinds of dye in these days."

"No!" His shock only appeared to be genuine.

She said, "Go to sleep."

"I'm not sure I can. You've given me a terrible burden of doubt that causes me to...wonder."

"Count the stunning sum of the national debt a thousand at a time and you'll go to sleep from exhaustion."

"The President's working on it."

"It's still stupendous. Try counting that high. I'll waken you in an hour."

"You're one of those regimented women who block out the day in duties and time. You need to be free to take life as it comes."

"I'll work on it."

He curled down on the wide, long seat and bunched the pillow under his head. The big, heavy comforter covered him very well. He smiled. And he thought how well that structured woman had adjusted to the day and to him. She was already "free" of structuring. She was really something.

He slept before he got to counting in the two hundred thousands. His snore was gentle and pleasant. She peeked over at him and smiled down on him like a guardian angel. She's been lucky.

So far.

The winds buffeted even that heavy, solid tractor cab. It made the bent connecting wheel between the cab and trailer groan, but Ruff slept on.

Meanwhile on the bed, Maggie was getting more basic instruction in male humor and imagination. Some of the artwork was simply, stunningly beautiful. Crass, yes, but the drawing and coloring were really lovely. Some were as crude as the, uh, jokes?

What all makes all sorts of people laugh? How interestingly basic is the male mind.

But she also found surprising innuendos. While the humor of it might go by the more basic male mind, it would tickle in those of other humors.

Maggie hadn't realized male humor could be subtle.

And she remembered male laughter shared where there had been nothing of humor to her. Males had a touchstone of understanding and also of humor that women didn't always share.

Maggie allowed Ruff to sleep longer than the hour, so he wakened, moving, stretching, pausing as he realized where he was. And she watched when he turned his head quickly to see if she was still there.

He relaxed.

He thought how interesting it was that when he saw she was still there, he relaxed. Why? Had he thought she'd have sneaked out of the cab and strode off through the wind-driven snow to find another shelter? Or was he relieved no one had snatched her away from him? It was then he realized she was his.

Now, how had he decided that? He wasn't ready for a commitment. He'd let Bets go because they were getting too serious. Why was he now pleased this Donner woman was still around?

She smiled at him slightly and said, "It's almost four."

He squinted his eyes and replied, "It just dawned on me that your name is Donner. Wasn't it the Donners who starved to death in the cold going to California?''

"Not this branch. We know that, in winter, high hills have snow on top of them. We stayed in heaven. We didn't need to go looking for it."

"That sounds like a practiced response. How many people have questioned you about Donner Pass?"

"Nowadays, most people pay it no mind? You're my fifth. No TEXAN inquires about the name. They know that since we have TEXAS, none of us would have any reason to try for California."

"How about Indiana?" he asked.

"I haven't really seen the ground." She looked at the fogged windows. "How can I tell?"

"Stick around. You'll find all kinds of things in Indiana."

"Ice and snow? Wind and subzero weather?"

He nodded. Then he had the gall to tell her, "It's stimulating."

"Stimulating?" She narrowed her eyes to "taste" the meaning of the word.

"Yeah, you don't have to wake up every morning just knowing it'll be *another* pretty day. Up here, before you even open your eyes, you feel the tingle of anticipation." He licked his lips because his mind had a sexual blip, but his tongue went bravely on, "You get up to look out the window to be surprised by a different new day."

"Hallelujah." Her tone was tolerant.

He went on in a dreamy fashion, "And we ice skate."

"Shucks, boy, we ice skate down in TEXAS!"

He slid a smug glance over as he finished, "In Indiana, we do it outside!" But "doing it" outside made his eyes sparkle and he had to control a salacious grin.

She smiled back as if he was being cheerful. "Where did you get a name like Ruffan Reddy?"

"The whole thing is Ruffan Urick Reddy. That makes the initials R. U. Reddy. My dad's name is Adam Marlin Reddy. A. M. Reddy."

"I see."

He bit his lower lip to keep from laughing. She was being so tolerant. He told her kindly, "It's really just a conversation piece. My dad told me that after I got used to my name, anything else would be easy."

And again she replied, "I see."

3

As the day darkened, the wind lessened but the cold was severe. The temperature was thirty-two degrees below zero. The windchill took the temperature down to sixty degrees below zero.

The radio told how cold it was and reminded families to bring their pets inside. Maggie instantly knew that would mean dogs. Cats would already be inside, curled by the stove or heating vents.

Listeners were advised to leave the cold water faucets running a minimum stream so that the pipes wouldn't freeze. And they were informed about potholes and burst tires.

People were told to stay inside. It was dangerously cold.

With some worry, Maggie asked Ruff, "How long can you run the motor?"

"I've got gas enough to sit here with the heat on until the day after tomorrow. But before then, we'll be rescued."

"And if we're not?" she asked. "We could freeze out here!"

"Naw. We could manage. The tractor's cab is tight, and we have the blankets." He looked at her with such logic. "I'll keep you warm."

Yeah.

The obscured daylight dimmed and the wind swirled the snow in the fading light.

Their supper was more cautious. He had another two sandwiches. He ate only half of one sandwich. That sobered her, for the supper was a two-sandwich supply. Instead of eating the portion of the sandwich that Ruff had left for her, she ate only a granola bar.

He scolded her. "Go ahead. Eat it. Your body needs the fuel. I can't have you freezing and shivering and grabbing my blankets to get cl—" He ran out of words as his mind registered vivid images of her naked body trying to get closer to his.

She was logical. "I have my grandfather's blanket and my jacket. I'll be fine."

"Haven't I told you that 'jacket' is a blouse?" He frowned at her. Then, really curious, he asked, "What did you think winter was like up here?"

She responded readily, "I did check the logistics. Winters in Indiana haven't been this way in twenty years!"

Ruff considered as he nodded. "You're right. But that is not a coat or even a jacket. You get the sheepskin coat. I'm hot enough." Yeah. He was so hot he could hardly move. And he was, by then, stripped down to just the long underwear, the turtleneck top and his jeans.

He'd gone into the back of the cab to shed the long underwear bottoms. He'd put his jeans back on. The tractor cab was warm enough for her. He couldn't save gas by turning the heat down. He liked looking at her in that... blouse.

She had on a silk turtleneck top under the jacket. The jacket was flannel lined and the outside was silk? She couldn't be wearing a bra. As she moved and turned, her breasts were free and moved that way. She probably didn't realize it.

She was so female. He loved the smell of her in his cab. It wasn't perfume. It was her...fragrance. It was subtle and really different from the odor of a man. If she left the cab, any man coming inside would inhale and know a woman had been there.

He was mesmerized as he watched Maggie, who was busy tidying up. She shared her caramels, giving him two because she knew he'd not eaten enough. They now had the granola bars, a whole sandwich and a quarter of one left to eat in the morning.

Outside the cab, the night was swallowing the swirls of snow. Maggie had the feeling they'd be there all of that night. The wind had eased, but she could still hear it as it blew in gusts and the visibility was very limited.

All of the day's seeming snowfall had been whipped up from the snow already on the ground. With the less strident winds, the snows stayed in lower swirls. It settled more so that, from the truck's high cab and through the lessening haze of the blown ground snow, the moon was apparent.

How strange to see the calm moon looking down on the taggle end of earth's natural turmoil.

With a gesture to the calming view, Ruff explained, "It's called redistribution. Snow is blown around by the wind, and piles up in unexpected places. Like our tax money in Washington.

"After Congress voted their own twenty-five thousand raise, us truck drivers have been trying to be the decision makers on our raises, but the companies aren't allowing it. Unlike Congress, we weren't elected to have control over our own lives and salaries like that."

"How rude."

He grinned at her response. He nodded and agreed, "It is."

So she asked, "How much do you think a truck driver should earn?"

"Earn? With the usage of that particular word, you're not talking equality of jobs here, you're talking work. Do you realize that? About fifty percent of the truckers own their own tractor. That's what this here part of the truck is called and we're sitting in the tractor's cab. The tractor owners are called owner-operators. They're responsible for the upkeep and care. It can get expensive.

"With trucking," Ruff explained, "we're almost always under the hammer of time. Everybody wants whatever they've ordered . . . yesterday."

She agreed with slightly lifted eyebrows, "Yes."

"I knew you were that type."

"There's another type?"

His eyes laughed at her as he said with serious emphasis, "We're still looking." But he was really just looking at her. He smiled in a friendly manner.

She was old enough to recognize male interest was enhanced by idleness, so she inquired, "Can you play double solitaire?"

He went along with it. He turned out an open hand in a gesture to reveal the real him and replied, "Name a card game, I can play it."

So they got out their two decks of cards and began again to distract him from their isolated circumstances.

But playing cards only showed what a cheerfully competitive sport she was, and it betrayed her humor and her acceptance of circumstances.

His head tilted back to show indifference, he asked with seeming casualness about her cards, "What've you got?"

She replied with great wisdom, "Gradually, gradually, you will see it all."

He choked.

So when someone shouted and pounded on the locked door, they glanced up at each other with a strange, disappointed poignancy.

Their rescuer had arrived.

Before they were ready to do so, they would leave their isolated island of potential enclosure, and go back to reality, to other people. They would lose this opportunity to share time together. It was finished?

Ruff leaned across her and opened her door to look down and say, "So you got—"

But the man huddled there was not a rescuer. He was a pathetic, shivering mass of limited humanity. His shoulders hunched, he told the two in the cab, "We're stuck down a way. I saw your lights when we went past. The car's engine died. I barely got it off the road. We have the baby with us."

"How far?" Ruff asked.

"It's that way." He didn't take his hands out of his pockets to gesture. He indicated the direction with his chin. He added earnestly, "Over the hill. I'm freezing."

The two marooned ones shifted, and they exchanged concerned looks.

The wayfarer climbed into the cab, closed the door and shivered violently as he huddled on the edge of the seat.

He said, "It's cold."

And Ruff's eyes slitted. "Which way is your car? You say you went past here?"

"It's on the other side. We were heading for Fort Wayne."

"How'd you see us?"

"When we passed you, the snow let up enough. We saw you were okay. The lights were on. God. I can't tell you how glad I am that you're here. We have no heat."

Was he telling the truth? He could be anything. He was shivering so hard that he was very convincing. How far had he come? Or was he only pretending?

Ruff thought the man expected him to go fetch his...family. What if there was no family? What if the man then took the truck and Maggie and drove off? Ruff said to her, "The tractor won't move. The wheel's stuck."

Maggie almost nodded. "You take the key."

Ruff considered their intrusive guest and shared his opinion with Maggie. "He's as cold as he says."

The man was shivering. He did hear. He said, "I'm no threat. None at all. My wife and kids are in the car." He repeated yet again, "I saw your lights." How important that had been to him. "I had to be sure we could get in your cab. Give me a minute. Can they come back here?"

The hosts both said, "Yes." But Ruff looked at Maggie very soberly.

And the man said again, "Just give me a minute. I'll go get them. She can't carry both of the kids."

Two kids? Were there really?

Ruff asked gently, "Where you from?"

Readily, his shivering voice responded, "We're from Georgia. I didn't know Indiana had weather like this anymore. The last time I was up here . . . it was in February that year, too, and it was sunny, jacket weather."

Ruff flipped on the CB and told their surprise guest, "I need to report on you." Then he said into the CB, "Claude? This is Ruff. We have a surprise guest—"

"What's going on?"

"Here, he can give you the particulars." Ruff turned the mouthpiece toward the man and said, "Give him the information. Name, home place, destination, the names of anybody who might be looking for you or worried about you."

Apparently, the man was legit. Still shivering, he managed to be clear as he said, "Malcolm and Audrey Millstone and our two children from Price, Georgia?"

The speaker said, "You don't sound much like a Georgian."

"We're originally from Illinois. That's where we were headed."

"Give me your license number."

Malcolm did that. Then he asked, "Where'd this storm come from? We didn't know you all were dealing with winters like this again."

Claude made a disgruntled sound and shut off.

As Ruff reset the microphone of the CB back to the driver's side, Malcolm said again, "We had no idea it could be this way. We weren't prepared."

Maggie felt the need to reassure the man's logic. "That's what I thought, too."

In some disgust, Ruff inquired, "Don't you guys ever watch the weather on TV?"

Ignoring the chiding, Maggie said, "Let's go get the others."

"Not you," Ruff said. "Him and me. Give him the sheepskin coat."

Her eyes big, Maggie looked at Ruff. She said very seriously, "Be careful."

He said, "I will." Then he said something strange. "Lock the doors until I get back. Don't open them for anybody else."

Maggie became very still. Ruff thought it might be a trick? That somebody was taking advantage of the storm and wanted the truck? And they might drag her out and hit her over the head and let her freeze? Or take her along…for a while? She nodded in tiny bobs. Seriously, she told Ruff again, "You be careful." Any man alone could be jumped by waiting men.

Ruff went over into the back and put on the long underwear and a heavy sweater with a knitted hood. Then he shrugged into a greatcoat.

He came back over the seat back and under the steering wheel. He looked around Maggie at the intruder. "How're you doing?"

"I'm ready. With this coat, it'll be easier. Thank you." Then he asked Maggie, "Will you be warm enough without it?"

She replied, "There's a blanket."

Ruff said to her, "I'll be back."

Sitting beside him on the seat, she was startled when he put his arms around her and, as he did, he put one of her hands into his coat pocket. She had been surprised by his movement and stiffened somewhat. His impulsive affection didn't seem in character. Then he insisted her hand go into the pocket, and she felt as he put the gun into her hand.

She leaned her head back and looked up into his face showing her surprise, then she frowned. If she had the gun, he would be unprotected.

He said softly, "Be quiet. And be careful. The password is TEXAS."

She said, "But—"

He nodded soberly, and as the other man went out the passenger side, Ruff said again, "Lock the doors.

I have a key. Get in the back on the floor if you don't hear the password." He leaned past her and locked that door, then he went out his door and stood until he heard her lock the door after him.

So she got to wait.

And wait.

She was in a strange place without any readily available help handy. There was the CB. She could shoot a gun.

She didn't want to have to do that. She wanted a whole and healthy Ruff back again. She didn't want anything to happen to him. It wasn't only because she was attracted to him, but that he was a good man. Nothing should happen to a good man. We need to preserve good men.

She got to wait longer. It was eerie. The dark appeared to press closer around the locked cab. There was no sound except for the cold wind with a slithering of ice sprinkles against the glass.

Maggie shivered. Where was Ruff? How long should she wait before she sent out the alarm? Who could respond?

While Ruff had the greatcoat, Malcolm had left with the wonderful shaggy sheepskin coat. There was no way she could go out into the cold, cold world with the jacket she wore.

If the whole premise was true, and they brought a baby there, how would they fit four more bodies into the cab?

She looked around. It shouldn't be too bad. Just overnight, and they'd all sleep. She and the woman could be in the back with the two kids. How could Ruff and a man share the front seat?

They'd both sit up all night.

She looked over at the bed. It wasn't big enough for two women and two kids.

So then she wondered what sort of kids they'd be. After they'd been dragged out of a freezing car and made to trudge across the snow and wind and get into the cab of a crowded truck, how would they be? And she felt some peripheral empathy for the woman and the kids.

What if the whole thing was as Ruff had suspected and they just wanted the truck? If there were other men, then they could detach the trailer from the crumpled wheel and take the cab...the tractor. It was worth a lot of money.

She had the gun. But what good would it do her without Ruff? What if they killed him or knocked him over the head to let him freeze and then came for the cab? As she'd been directed to do, she got into the back of the cab and lay on the bed with the gun in her hand and the safety off.

It seemed forever before they came. Ruff hollered, "Hey, TEXAS! Open the door locks."

She put the safety on the gun and scrambled over the back onto the seat and unlocked both doors.

The wind came in from the east door with Ruff and out the west door as their guests hurried inside. The cold filled the cab. A little girl was swung up onto the cab seat, and she looked appalled.

She huddled down in the middle of the seat and hid her face against the WWII blanket. A yelling baby was handed up next, and Maggie took it. It had soiled diapers and smelled to high heaven.

Then a woman came in, her teeth chattering. She swung her snowy feet along and got over into the back without being told. She took the baby to her. The two men clambered inside and slammed the doors.

No one said anything but sounds. The baby yelled bloody murder. The stench from the diaper was just about overwhelming.

Malcolm was sitting, hunched over, shivering, taking the little girl back inside his coat with him, warming her.

Ruff struggled out of his coat, and Maggie helped. She slid the gun from her hand into his, and he put it into the pocket of his coat, looking at her to be sure she knew where it was.

Still? He still thought these frozen guests could be a threat? It had happened. It could? She judged the four and allowed Ruff to be the careful one.

After a time, Maggie turned to kneel on the edges of the front seats and reached over to bring the screaming baby to her. She peeled back the blankets on the bed enough to get the sheet. She told Audrey, "Diapers."

But Audrey said, "Ask Malcolm."

"Malcolm? Diapers?"

He put a hand inside the little girl's top shirt and pulled out several diapers. The diapers had been used as insulation for the little girl. Malcolm was in something like a chill shock. He wasn't functioning really well.

With the screaming baby on her lap, Maggie undid the thick satin sack that held the child. Then Maggie got down to the flowered corduroy pants on the baby and finally reached the diaper. She opened and folded it back under the baby's cold bottom. Using a handkerchief handed her by Ruff, Maggie wiped the baby's bottom.

Then Maggie put a clean, sister-warmed diaper on the little one and redid her clothing. The baby still yelled, so Maggie put the baby inside her jacket and held her close, humming softly to her. The baby was so cold that Maggie was chilled.

Ruff had taken the dirty diaper and soiled handkerchief and pitched them out the door. One can't always be tidy.

But he took the greatcoat and put it over Maggie and the baby. Maggie made certain the baby's nose was free, and she went on humming. The cold baby was like ice to Maggie's rapidly cooling body.

The poor little baby had been so cold and so uncomfortable that she cried for a time, but less and less. Then the mother tapped Maggie on the shoulder and handed her a pacifier. The woman's hand was like ice.

No wonder she allowed Maggie to take care of the child. Audrey was so chilled that she wouldn't have been able to warm the child, while Maggie could. Maggie's body warmth and the pacifier did the trick. Having first quietened, the baby then slept.

Ruff eased them over onto him, supporting Maggie and watching over her. And with the heat of Ruff around her, gradually Maggie warmed.

After a long time, Malcolm eased from the sheepskin coat. Maggie helped him pull it from behind him and he covered himself and the little girl on his lap.

Finally, they all slept or dozed.

Once, Maggie was aware. Sometime or the other, Ruff had lowered the lights inside the cab. And he'd lowered the sound on the CB.

When the baby shifted, Maggie roused a little. But what charmed her most of all was that Ruff then moved his arms and hands to soothe *her!*

Was he that used to sleeping with a woman?

Of course, their sleeping arrangements did amuse Maggie. She'd thought the little family would sleep on the bed. Everyone but the mother was in the front seat of the cab! How'd the woman arrange that? Clever.

But the baby felt so good against her chest. The little body was finally toasty warm and her little mouth suckled the pacifier sporadically. Apparently she wasn't any the worse for the adventure.

And the little girl slept. Malcolm coughed. The mother was silent.

Maggie sighed and moved a little against Ruff's shoulder and chest.

Next to her ear, Ruff asked softly, "You okay?"

She moved her head up to look at his face and smiled groggily at him.

He brought his big hand up and just lay it on the side of her head, holding it to him. He whispered, "You're really something."

And she whispered back, "So're you."

Then she minutely rubbed the other side of her face against his chest—and went back to sleep.

Morning came bright and bitterly cold. The wind had stilled so that the snow lay pleasantly on the ground. But the cold was silent and very wicked. It was like a huge still monster, which waited for human stupidity.

Maggie stretched and started to move. Then she grabbed her chest in alarm. The baby was gone! She gasped and her head jerked as she looked around, but Ruff made a rumble in his chest as he shifted and soothed her with his hands.

Maggie knew as Ruff wakened because his breathing changed. It was audible in the silent cab. Across the seat Malcolm still slept.

His lap was empty. He had a blanket draped across him. He was sprawled so that he had to be warm.

Maggie moved minutely, stretching up to see.

Ruff's hands pulled back slightly, not wanting her to do that. Not wanting her to leave him.

Maggie continued to stretch her neck until she could see the bed, and there the mother was, under the blankets, curled on her side with the baby against her. The little daughter was close by. All were covered with the blankets—and the sheepskin coat.

Maggie slowly, silently, turned her head and looked at Ruff. He had a pillow behind his head. His eyes were serious. He watched Maggie.

She smiled and mouthed, "Good morning."

He pulled her to him and settled her back against him. Then he tilted her mouth to his, and he kissed her.

It was a very sweet, gentle kiss. But his breathing roughened and was high in his chest. He licked his lips and breathed through his mouth.

It was then with a determined sound of unopposable strength that the snowplows came through, shoving back the blown snow. They'd been busy most of the night. The roads were clear. With the roads cleared, a couple of trucks but only one car passed. There was not much traffic.

Their rescuers came. Knowing about the additional people, it was a van. And the hosts had to waken their guests. There was the reluctance to get cold again. The little girl's name was Susan. She was uncertain and wrapped her arms around her daddy's neck.

The Millstones repeated their urgent thank-yous. "You saved our lives."

The sheepskin coat was on Audrey, who carried the baby wrapped against her. Ruff put the greatcoat around Maggie and held her arm as if someone might take her away from him. He told her, "Stay with me until the tractor is freed."

Maggie readily agreed, "I should see about the papers in my car."

As the transfer of the Millstones to the van was completed, and goodbyes and gratitudes given, the van's driver assured Ruff, "I'll get your coat back."

As that was going on, another trucker came along to help Ruff. And Maggie was put back into the tractor cab. That annoyed the van driver, who'd saved the front seat for Maggie.

The van driver left with the Millstones waving. And Maggie thought, the Millstones were so frozen, they'd only remember a trucker rescued them. They'd forget which one and love all truckers.

That wouldn't be such a bad thing to happen.

The connector wheel between the tractor and the trailer was a wheel that allowed the tractor to turn, and the trailer to follow. That wheel had been warped when the tractor slid unevenly over the frozen snow, crashing into her car and then into the bank of frozen snow. It was rather difficult to get the tractor free. But there on the side of the road—in the still, bitter cold— the two men did accomplish it.

Ruff shoveled a path over to the door of Maggie's car. From her glove compartment, she took the things she needed to report the accident. She took out the registration and insurance papers. There was also the book on how to repair any of the car's problems. Maggie figured that saving the book was probably a waste of effort.

As she left the crumpled car, she considered the blessing of the seat belt and the headrest. Then she looked back at Ruff, who was working around his tractor. And she thought of the care he'd given her and the Millstone family. He really was a king of the road.

But then, women tended to become attached to a male who was a help. No matter who. Perhaps it was their husband, a doctor, their lawyer or a trucker who had rescued them.

Something a woman had to work at... like a recalcitrant window or a door that stuck, men could solve so easily. It was worthwhile to have a man around.

Maggie stood there in Ruff's greatcoat and was warm. She was an independent woman who traveled alone. She was responsible for where the several film companies filmed their pictures. She was a site scout. They depended on her.

So how come she was all wishy-washy over being allowed to share the tractor cab of a truck after the driver of it had wrecked her car?

There was that. And she was amused by the conflict of dependence and independence.

4

Ruffan Reddy drove the tractor as if he had been born driving something like that. He and Maggie Donner were on their way to a truck stop, five miles east of the highway.

Ruff told Maggie, "While it's the nearest place, it has a great truck maintenance area and any needed truck parts available. There's enough room so that trucks can turn around easily and idle or park. There's space."

Watching Ruff, Maggie observed the ease with which he handled the only mobile fragment left from the wreck. She grieved over the demise of her first, self-purchased automobile. It had been her first major purchase. That she could buy her own car had given her a feeling of controlling her own life.

Then, too, she found she was a little sad to leave the hiatus his temporarily idled cab had supplied for them. How else would she have come to know such a man?

She glanced over at Ruff and considered how clever he was to be able to manipulate such a cumbersome, oddly shaped vehicle. He was a king of the road.

Maggie asked, "Since we already know about your father and his strange manner of being named and of naming you, what is your mother like?"

"She's calm."

Maggie had to put her head back to laugh, and he kept glancing over to see that and still watch the road. The access road was cleared, but it hadn't been swept and tidied. Trucks could handle it. Cars were a different vehicle altogether. This road was for trucks.

The five miles didn't take long. And it was immediately obvious why it was a truck stop. The gas station area was different. It was roomily made for trucks. Across the way, there was a restaurant/store. And there were several cabins. The entire layout was utilitarian. No frills.

To her brief dismay, the cabins were full. But Ruff said, "There's room in the cab. Don't worry about it. Since my truck hit your car, I'm responsible for you and I'll take care of you."

To hear such talk was amusing for such an independent woman. She had been on her own since she graduated from college almost four whole years before then. But she had been taught manners. She smiled when she said, "Thank you."

As he slid the tractor into the indicated slot, Ruff's lashes closed down as he glanced at her. She thought he looked a little like an unhungry fox watching a mouse.

She was not a mouse.

But she had agreed to sleep in his cab with him. Just what sort of woman did a thing like that?

Well, she had no option. She had no transport. The cabins were already filled. She would have to sleep somewhere. She was adrift. No car, no place to go. And Ruff had promised to show her great background for the film crew. She looked around differently.

This truck stop wasn't it. But then again, maybe for another film? She took instant pictures of it from all angles. Drivers willingly posed.

Between photo sessions, she called the Indy branch of her insurance people and got a busy signal. So she faxed the truck stop pictures to her office to be filed and paid with her credit card.

She did get to the pressed insurance agent. He would send out someone to check out her car. If it was indeed totaled, her insurance covered a rental. She could have nineteen dollars a day on a rental. The car would be delivered to her. It might take another day. He hoped she understood.

She did.

Then Ruff took her into the building from which there was a loud sound of country music and mostly male laughter. Ruff told her, "I thought you might need supplies. There's a better choice for females since we've got so many women driving trucks."

The building was one story and adequate. The ladies' room was pristine and there were showers. In the main section of the restaurant, there were booths and an open space for dancing.

A man asked Ruff, "You know her?"

Ruff said, "Yeah. She's with me."

The man pushed his lower lip up as he contemplated Maggie. They were not introduced.

Ruff put her on the other side of him the way a basketball player shifts the ball to dribble past an opponent. She was comparable to a basketball? He was possessive?

Then Ruff took her to the product-jammed area that sold female supplies. With patience in searching, a looker could find just about everything. There was a stunning supply of labeled conversation piece sweatshirts. And there was a rack of paperback books. She browsed and bought five books.

Ruff stood patiently waiting for her. He suggested she get a good jacket, and he tried several on her before he chose what she would need.

Maggie mentioned, "It's too big."

He slid his eyes over her as he said through his teeth, "You're gonna be wearing a thick sweatshirt under this."

She stood straight and looked off out the front windows to the tire-marked snow. She replied, "I'm going back to TEXAS in just about two days?" She questioned to see if he understood such a simple thing.

"The jacket and sweatshirt will preserve you so that you can live long enough to leave."

But just then a heavy voice called, "Hey, that you, Ruff? Got a coat here for you. That old sheepskin."

"Thanks." And Ruff went over to retrieve his coat. He came back with it. He looked at her seriously. He told her, "You can take this along and send it back when you get home."

"You are really sweet, but I don't actually need it. I'll get a rental car when they can find someone to drive it up here." She asked him, "What do the truckers do if their tractors aren't available and they want to go someplace else?"

"They call ahead and have something here for them."

She said a defeated, "Oh." Then she asked, "How do I get around here to see the area?" And she waited to see if he'd suggest she drive the rental back up there.

He replied, "Today, I'm planning on taking you around. We'll have lunch at a nice place not far from here. In three days, you can see the whole area."

"But how can you take the time—now?"

"I have to get the trailer back in working order and take it for a load that'll be ready by then. I'll have the time."

Maggie suspected he was deliberately being available. He shouldn't. There was no way she'd hang around up there in that area freezing, either that winter or especially for any extended time. She'd seen a TV special about how the next ice age would cover this area first. She hadn't realized it had already started.

Maggie told Ruff gently, "The ice age has started."

But he rejected her information with laughter. He was so amused.

Her new sweatshirt declared that she was from IN-DIANA. They were nudging it to make the state all in caps, mimicking TEXAS. People in Indiana are pushy.

She wore the sheepskin coat, which was too large for her even with the bulky Indiana sweatshirt. Her new gloves and higher boots were synthetic materials and attractive.

With her dressed to his satisfaction, the twenty-six-hour acquaintances went out to explore the countryside—in Ruff's tractor cab.

She had her camera.

He knew exactly where to go and what pictures she should take from where and which angle.

She turned to him once and said, "You have a very good eye."

His lashes heading in her direction, he smiled slightly and replied, "Yeah."

When they returned to the truck compound, her crumpled car had been dragged into the edge of the motor yard and temporarily abandoned until someone came and certified that it had become junk. Think about that. A car made in TEXAS by TEXANS. The very idea caused a pang.

As she anguished over it, Ruff said, "I'm just glad you weren't hurt." He said that as he put his big hand on the back of her neck.

"What about your trailer?"

"It's gonna need some help. I'm waiting for them to see if they can send another trailer to load."

"I am so sorry I caused you to crash."

"I told you, it was my fault. I shouldn't of overrun you. I should have been paying more attention." Then in a denial of lack of attention, he asked, "Do you see that church? In the snow, that way, it's real pretty. Without the snow, it's not much."

By then she asked *him*, "How should I take this one?"

"I'll go to the other side and drive back so you can take a run of pictures. The trees in front of it'll be nice. They're all bare and look like a delicate screen. Then you'll come out there and it'll be clear for a while before you get to the next screening trees."

"I suspect you're better at this than I am."

"I love the countryside. I look at it all along the trips. This country is such a range of landscapes. It's really wondrous."

She asked with curiosity, "Would you be interested in exploring backgrounds the way I'm doing?"

Ruff shrugged minutely. "I've never thought about doing it."

"You ought to consider it. I could introduce you around in my company. They need somebody to recommend settings. I'll give you a list of people to contact. Do you have a camera?"

"Naw."

"The cameras now are just—" Ruff had turned the tractor around and paused on the deserted byway. She told him, "This is perfect. Let me start here. Ease along."

As the run was finished, she said to him, "Great. That's just right. *Ahhh*. You are brilliant!" She turned and grinned at him.

Then she logged the shot in her books. She gave the location, the time, the date and how the run was done in what vehicle.

She took a deep breath and looked around. "I'm so glad you ran into me. I would never have found this place. And all this snow."

Then she looked at her watch. "I've taken up your entire afternoon."

His comment leaped ahead into the evening. He reminded her, "All the cabins are filled."

"Yes." She adjusted to planning for later. "You did say that I can sleep in the cab? Just for tonight. I get the seat. You have the bed. It's just for tonight. I ought to be able to get down to Indy tomorrow."

"There're a couple of other places you ought to see before you go. The light is better, midday. Don't run away too soon. There's more."

More? More...what? She did glance over at him. But he was seriously looking at the snowy road ahead.

She said, "I need to compensate you for the time and gas for the ca—for the tractor."

"I'll give you a bill."

"Good! I was wondering if you'd allow me. Thank you for being so businesslike on this. Now I feel free to use you. May we go past the old school again?"

He was still recovering from her saying she could use him. But he did push up his lower lip and frown. Then he said, "The light's not right."

"Wellll. It would give them an idea."

He glanced over at her. "We can do it, but we'd have to do it again tomorrow. It's supposed to snow again."

"*Great!*" And she laughed. "I don't see much snow, down in TEXAS. This is a treat." Then she added judiciously, "Would it be crass to want it a tad warmer?"

"Crass."

"Okay. Let it freeze then and ruin all the crops and pipes and what all."

"The land is used to it. Some crops do better if the weather is this cold."

"How rude to need it cold. Think of the miracle of an inside bathroom. I suppose that is mentioned now and again?"

"Most of the people now farming have had indoor plumbing all their lives." Then he admitted, "But even now, farmers generally have an emergency outhouse."

They went to the old, red-brick-sided, peaked slate-roofed, one-room school. Ruff parked, and they got out. It was good to walk around. In the last two days, they'd been so long in the cab that they were still stretching and moving their cramped muscles.

The old school had been salvaged at one time, but it was again in disrepair. Attention had been distracted from it, and no real use for it had been discovered.

The nosy couple went inside. The blackboard was real slate and vulgar words had been chalked there.

His eyes slid over to see her reaction, but like mice, she didn't "see" vulgarities.

She was so different. He stopped her and held her to him. That surprised her even as her body was delighted. They really didn't yet know each other well enough. She didn't object. But while she only put her hands on his upper arms, she lay her head sideways on his shoulder, facing out and not available to a kiss.

He knew she had on too many clothes. He said to her, "We need to get back so you can get in line for the phone and call whoever you need to contact."

"Okay. Thank you for helping me out...all the way along these last two days."

"My pleasure."

They went out to the tractor and climbed up into the cab.

He could not restrain his question, which had flooded his mind and tittered on the tip of his tongue all the while. After he'd driven along in silence, he finally asked, "Is any one of your calls to a particular man?"

She looked over at him and almost smiled. "No."

"Well, now." And he relaxed and his smile widened. Then he turned and grinned at her.

She said cautioningly, "I like TEXAS."

"You've mentioned that."

They'd known each other for almost thirty-six hours. That was not a basis for anything. Thoughtfully, she said, "I probably shouldn't sleep in the cab tonight." She licked her lips and added, "I might ruin your reputation. You have to see these men all the time, here and there. And since I've listened to your CB, I understand they do tend to chatter."

"You already know you have to stay with me tonight. There's no room anyplace around. I asked. Maybe the truckers will begin leaving tomorrow.

Then, by tomorrow night, you can sleep in a real bed. Did I tell you about the old motel over in Spencerville? It goes back to the Civil War and—"

She corrected courteously, "It was a War Between the States. It was a war about control. It really *was* federal control against states' rights. The only reason the North threw in the slavery issue—three years into the war—was because England and France were about to join the South. They needed cotton for their mills. The charge of slavery was the blockade against England and France coming into the war on the side of the South. Not many Southerners had slaves, and that issue wouldn't have caused the Southern loyalty to back such a war."

He said, "I've never heard that explanation."

"Honey, that's 'cause you're a Yankee? But I'd bet you know about Yankee dimes?"

"Okay, what's a Yankee dime?"

She lifted her eyebrows and supplied the answer, "A kiss."

"We pulled that on those fragile Southern women?"

"Young girls."

"No!" He was wonderfully aghast.

"Yep. My great-granny told me so."

"Shame on her."

"She got it from *her* granny."

"Yankees wouldn't hoodwink nice young girls with a trick like that. It's probably something that's been altered with time."

And she slid in, "Just like saying the War Between the States was about slavery. The real reason—states' rights—is now ignored."

"Let's see. There's a good word to put in here. It's a...sword touch."

She agreed. "You've just said it...touché."

"I think you're smarter'n me."

"You say that, having just shown me wonderful places that will make great backgrounds for films. You see what's around you. And you know people better than I. You drive wonderfully."

"That's said by a woman that I ran down on a highway."

"I was lucky you did. I'd have probably frozen to death. My heater was just about nil, and I was fiddling with it, trying to get more heat."

"Good. I've got that down for my defense."

"I've told you all along, the wreck was my fault."

"Not this time, honey." His voice was soft. Then he said, "It's about suppertime. I know you're hungry. My stomach can outgrowl yours anytime. That blank-looking truck stop has the best food you've ever eaten. Let's go back and be early."

"I'll buy."

"Okay."

She was delighted. "Thank you."

"For what?"

"For letting me treat you to supper."

"I don't have an expense account, and you probably do." He was pretending to be poor and giving her the feeling of control.

"Yes. And I can put your gas on my tab, too. I really appreciate you taking the time to show me around. I would never have found those places."

"Sure you would. But I liked showing them to you."

"Thank you."

"You're welcome. Are we going to go on being this polite?"

She looked at him in surprise and exclaimed, "Of course!"

His smothered laugh was poorly done.

The meal was trucker fare of roast meat, potatoes, gravy, carrots and peas and bread and butter with jam. It was delicious. The bread was homemade and thick. The crust was chewy and the butter melted on it. *Ahhhhh.* Then there was the choice of pie slices...with homemade ice cream.

Knowing full well she shouldn't, Maggie ate her share. She had to discreetly undo the button on her pants waist. She was stuffed. She was exquisitely casual, but she did smother burps.

Ruff had the gall to inquire, "Eat too much?"

"How crass of you to notice."

"I did, too, but I'll tell you, it's a good thing. We do the Indiana Two-step here for half the night, and it takes so much—"

"Indiana... two-step? You must mean the TEXAS two-step?"

"No. They stole it from us."

"Now, just a minute!"

And the whole place became embroiled in an argument over that very thing. Everybody else was on Indiana's side, while there was only one driver and Maggie vowing it was TEXAS that had started the two-step.

Ruff looked at the man who sided so positively with Maggie and gave him a warning stare. The guy smiled and licked his lips.

Maggie asked the guy. "Are you a TEXAN?"

He admitted, "I've drove through the whole state, from Loozeeanna to El Paso!" His name was Tom.

She applauded and nodded with somber agreement. "That'll do it."

Under the hullabaloo, Ruff said to Maggie, "He's called more than just Tom. He's a tomcat. Watch out for him."

So Tom said, "Let's show them how it's done." Since he didn't say what, that could be taken just about any way and there were cries and laughs and hubbub.

But looking at Tom, Ruff rose slowly and put his hand on Maggie's chair as he said to Tom, "No. I'm her partner."

Maggie got up and took Ruff's hand. Under her breath, she said, "I do hope you know how to two-step?"

He advised, "Start easy."

Hell. He knew everything. He slid his glance over to her through those eyelashes and he smirked. He strutted and showed off, and he showed her off. He was wickedly smug.

Everybody was dancing by then in lines or with partners. Some of the guys played the female part and were so funny.

As they walked along to the music before he turned her, Maggie said to Ruff, "I've heard of shy men just like you."

And he had the gall to reply, "Yeah."

The evening was nice. There was laughter and hoots and a great turmoil of talk and brag. It was a really delightful, animated evening. It was one of the few times there were more men than women dancing. With the TEXAS two-step, you didn't need a partner.

And all that while, Maggie had a small recorder to tape the sounds. She put it on her belt. It looked like a woman's change purse. That way, the filmmakers could be instructed on actual talk and sounds.

The dancing was a lot of fun. But bedtime did come.

The hero and his partner used the separate rest rooms. Then they got their jackets and were as discreet as they could be, walking out through the aisles of products. But they were seen.

There were a lot of watchers. The men knew the cabins were filled. They saw the pair walk out of the store and go across the snow under the big, high lights and beyond to Ruff's tractor cab. They watched as Ruff helped Maggie climb the steps into the cab. The watchers made no comment or sound. They were silent.

Maggie found the cab was warm. The motor was running. She asked, "When did you start the motor?"

"When you went to 'wash your hands' a while ago."

That was the excuse she'd used. The way he said it showed the quotation marks.

He soothed her. "I like a clean woman."

What was she to reply to that? He might just be making conversation. While she had never slept with a man, she felt the time was ripe. She would be intrigued to sleep with this man. But while he had been sure she knew he was not married, he could have a string of women clear across the whole country!

She was given pause by the reality that she didn't know him well enough to inquire as to his commitments. That alone ought to nudge her into being modest and quiet.

What if— Well, she would wait and see if there was a "what if"....

He didn't climb up after her. He gave her the sheepskin coat and said, "Put that over the bed. You might be warmer." Then he told her, "Lock the doors, I'll be back in about twenty minutes. Okay?"

She looked down at him. In the reflection of the lights, his face turned up, to watch her, was young and open. He probably wasn't a virgin, but he wasn't indiscriminate, either. He was giving her time to get into bed by herself. Alone. He would probably sleep across the seats.

A gentleman. A man who was gentle.

Without replying, she went on into the cab and closed the door. She locked it and tested the other door. Then she crawled over into the back where her suitcase was, and she retrieved her TEXAS flannel gown. That meant the flannel wasn't as serious as Yankee flannel.

She smeared cream on her face and wiped it with tissues, then she brushed her teeth. And she knew she'd sleep. She was really tired.

She crawled into the bed and pulled the covers over her. She would stay awake until Ruff came back.... How strange. She'd almost said, "—back home."

The cab was a home away from home. Even in that short time, it was a haven for her. More so than her car had ever been. That was probably because the tractor cab was wide enough and so high off the ground. One felt secure there.

Like a king of the mountain?

She yawned hugely. Her eyelids were heavy. Her stomach was still full and contented. She gradually relaxed into a deep sleep.

It was the full twenty minutes he'd promised her before Ruff came back. He unlocked the door and climbed into the cab. Almost immediately he realized she was actually asleep. She wasn't pretending.

He looked at her for a long time. Then he opened a window a half inch. He stripped down to his long johns, and he crawled into the other side of the bed.

Why not? She'd never know. She adjusted a little and made an *M* sound or two, and slept on. She was completely relaxed.

Ruff knew he had to sleep and not watch her or he wouldn't be able to stay in the cab. So he turned his back to her and did the entire multiplication table. Then he went over the route through L.A. after the earthquakes had altered roads. And eventually, he, too, slept.

5

Maggie wakened and began a marvelous stretch. Then she stopped abruptly as she realized she was lying on Ruff's arm and his face was about three inches from hers. He was in bed with her. He was wide-awake and watching her with intense concentration. She had his entire attention.

Behind him, between the bed and the cab seat, a curtain had been drawn. Their seclusion was extremely intimate.

"How'd you get here?" She asked that obvious question.

He replied in a husky voice, "It's my bed."

She couldn't argue that. She looked off to one side. Then she looked up into his blue eyes and she said, "I thought it would be easier for you to sleep across the front seat over there."

He minimally shook his head in denial.

"I didn't mean to usurp you."

"You sure as hell have done something drastic to me."

"What?"

His rough, breathy voice said, "You're in my arms, in bed, and you haven't even kissed me yet."

She said a soft, "Oh."

So her lips were just right, and he did kiss her. It was spectacular. Whew! Bursting shells and the whole shebang.

When his mouth left hers with tiny myriad sounds that were very erotic, she said, "My goodness."

And he replied with the Mae West classic, "Goodness has nothing to do with it."

She laughed in a very soft, intimate manner. Then she immediately knew what her parents had been doing over in their room, when her mother had laughed that soft way in the night. One never considers one's parents being... intimate. Of course, if they hadn't been, she wouldn't have been around to have heard her mother laugh that way.

Maggie looked at the man holding her, watching her so intently, and she said, "This is very warm and nice."

"I'm sweating."

"Are you ill?" She put her hand on his very hot forehead.

"I'm sick with love."

"Bosh!" she denied it. "How could you possibly say that."

"It's true. I've seen you under just about any circumstances a man should see a woman just since the day before yesterday. You're really something."

"I'm female."

"I had noticed that."

"No, I mean you're male and I'm female—"

"Yeah."

"—and we're sharing a bed, so your libido is going into overdrive because you've been trapped with me for a while and you just need release. You are not attracted to an individual. Any woman would do."

He nodded in serious little bobs and didn't say anything in case anything he would say might be wrong. He just watched her face with riveted attention.

She told him, "I'm not interested in you in that way."

"Otherwise, I'm not interested, either."

"Good. I'm glad. You can now behave and help me not to be interested in you."

He leaned his head back a trifle and narrowed his eyes. "So you are interested."

She flung out a hand. "Who would believe this conversation?" And she laughed such a bubble of humor.

Again he thought how different she was.

She said, "We could chat about the last few days and wonder how the Millstones are doing by now. Did you notice, right away, those people had the perfect name of a millstone?"

Undistracted, he replied, "No."

She observed, "This is very comfortable. It's too bad you're so intense. If you could relax, it would be easier and more pleasant."

His words came quickly, "I know how to get relaxed."

She laughed. She tried to smother it, and her green eyes spilled with humor but she blushed.

He guessed, "Now you're going to tell me you've never done it."

She shrugged, and they were so close he could feel that quite shiveringly. She admitted, "I haven't."

"Then it's time you did."

Her words were like those of a stadium seat partner. She invited, "Just as a ballpark figure, mind you, would you like to hear how many times I've been told that?"

"No."

"You don't want to know?" She was surprised.

He was honest. "I don't want to think of any other man holding you like this and wanting you like I want you, right now."

She looked into his eyes without crossing hers and told him earnestly, "I didn't mean to make it ha— difficult for you."

He pulled her body closer and curled his hip against her hip. "Feel."

The most remarkable thrill went through her body, overwhelming her. She gasped and shivered in erotic arousal. She said, *"Uhhhh—"* And then she breathed brokenly. How could she? She was a woman in control. She was plastered against him while he was gently nuzzling his prickly face against her neck by her shoulder, sending goose bump thrills skittering around in her.

She gasped and tried to solve her breathing problem as her body moved in little twitches against his.

What was she doing! She was just like a cat in heat! How shocking. How embarrassing. How...lovely....

Her fingers dug into his shoulders. His rooting face left her shoulder and his mouth sought hers and she—helped!

She did!

She didn't even think about what she was doing or how to go about it or if she should! She just went on and ... cooperated!

Before she really knew what was happening, she was out of her flannel nightgown and stark staring naked. But so was he! He was trembling! His hands shook as his muscles tightened, keeping him from scrubbing his hands over her hungrily.

And her hands on his back were thrilled by the knotted muscles roiling under his hot flesh. Think of the power of a man.

And his mouth slid down her chest and found her nipple. He nuzzled her gently, moving his scratchy face in slow, delicate swirls until she moved in sinuous writhings and her breathing changed. Then he suckled strong and wickedly marvelously so that her toes curled, and the bottoms of her feet tingled, and low inside her stomach was rampant want.

She gasped and shivered and moaned. She did that? And as she gasped and breathed, she considered she was really quite shocking. Her breaths were erratic and her hands were pulling his body closer when he was already as close as he could get, just about.

So she was really easy to turn over onto her back and apparently her knees automatically opened to receive him.

She was aware she'd done that, and she didn't correct the mistake and close her thighs.

He lay partially on her, conscious of her restless knees as he made love to her mouth and to her breasts. His hands moved down and caressed the delicate flesh of her inner thigh, encouraging her, stimulating her libido to excess and thrilling her wildly.

The roughness of his worker hands against the satin of her skin stirred her passions stunningly. And the texture of his body hair was thrilling to her bare flesh. She was making sounds of need. Her breaths were of passion and her writhings betrayed her want.

He loved it.

In his intimate pettings, he discovered the presence of her maidenhead. He became motionless in shocked surprise. She was new for him. He had to get her frantic or it would be too fast. He had never had a virgin. Obviously, she had never had a man.

He was already about out of his mind. He'd been very uncertain of her response. To find such a hot woman who was also a virgin at...twenty-*six?*...was impossible, wasn't it? He didn't pause to figure it out or to question her.

Then he battled with his conscience. Should he? She'd been pure all this time. This was a hot woman and she'd been careful. Should he take advantage of his amazing opportunity?

His body was emphatic. Every man deserved one. He was a man. He deserved being first with her. He kissed her his killer kiss and eased carefully into her blocked opening—to just feel it all—first. That was his intention. But he'd underestimated her reaction to him.

In a hoarse voice, he urged, "Help me to be careful. I don't want to hurt you."

She paused and didn't move. Her breathing was erratic, and her hands on his back were still.

That boggled him. Hadn't she realized what was happening? What he would do? To her? With her?

She groaned and said, "I can't wait any longer. You'll just have to brace yourself!"

The thrill of the shock went right through his chest and into his lightning rod.

She wrapped herself around him and curled her hips up as she moved so wondrously, so marvelously, so amazingly, so *wildly*, that he couldn't hold back.

But neither could she!

Their passion exploded into rampant hunger. Locked together, they strained to get closer. Their rhythm matched and they groaned and gasped in what had to be deadly combat.

Struggling, they rode that glory trail together to the peak, to a thundering pause. Then they shuddered into the convulsion and slid all the way...down...the other side.

They lay in an abandoned pile, the discarded covers strewn over and off the bed. The depleted pair lay panting and gasping. They couldn't focus their eyes.

Their hands sort of flopped as they attempted to re-assure each other after such a cataclysmic happening.

He finally heaved up onto one elbow and bent over her, smoothing her sweat-wet hair back from her face. "I'm sorry."

She opened her eyes and tried to focus. "Why?"

Trying to soften his gasping breaths, he told her, "I should have... been more... careful."

She closed her eyes and smiled such a smug, contented smile. She was outrageous.

So he kissed her. He kissed her softly to show he cared about her. Then he moved his hands on her. Soothingly, of course. But the kisses and the soothing got out of... hand, and he did the whole thing again.

She laughed. Such a soft, wicked laugh. He rubbed her face with his sweaty, whiskered face, and he was a little rough. He knew she couldn't climax again so soon. She was his. His feeling wasn't love as much as it was possession. She was his.

As he lay lax on her sweet body, his conscience did regard responsibility. He said, "I'll marry you."

"Why?"

A logical question. There they were in bed in the back of a tractor cab, having known each other going on three days. Why would he marry her? Because she was the most wonderful woman in the entire universe? Yeah. She was. But he needed to soothe her fears. He hadn't used a condom. While they were both safe from any communicable disease, she wasn't safe from being pregnant.

What a dumb thing to have done. He'd just lost it there. And she'd been so eager, so willing! If he'd insisted on the condom, she could have cooled. And she might well have changed her mind.

Excuses, excuses. He really hadn't made a decision. He'd just gone ahead, carried into paradise with her. It had been paradise. It had been as any man dreams it will be, and it is so rarely. Sex is that way. Ask any man. But even when it's bad, it's good.

Of course, sex is always good. It's just that sometimes it's better and on occasion, it can be spectacular.

He had just had the best ever. That magic moment. He owed her. He said again, "Don't worry. I'll marry you."

And again she inquired of him, with obvious curiosity, "Why?"

Ruff was amazed by her questioning. How could she ask why? Any woman jumped at the chance to get married. Men were meal tickets. Easy...

Well, he had to admit that there were a whole lot of women who worked after they got married. Would this nubile woman leave their babies at home and hire a woman to take care of them? Them? When had the urge to be a daddy crept up on bachelor Ruffan Reddy?

Just in the last couple of days.

Right now, he knew more about her than he had any other female. Look how she'd reacted to her car being run over by a truck. She hadn't come apart. She'd been calm and practical. She hadn't sworn or cried or scolded him. She had never blamed him, at all.

Just being able to watch her take care of that baby, the other night, had been special. For him to see her cleaning it, warming it, showed him she was tender and earnest. Her face had been so sweet. And he remembered her alarm when she'd wakened and found the baby was gone.

It had been his own hands that had lifted the baby from Maggie and given it back to its mother. Audrey Millstone had checked—how many times—when she was still shivering under all those blankets and even after Malcolm had insisted she also take the sheepskin coat.

For a while after that, Audrey's body had been cooler than the baby's. When she finally warmed up enough, she'd wanted her baby back. And the sleeping Maggie trusted Ruff so much, even then, that she hadn't wakened when he'd eased the baby from her and given the kid to its mother.

And now Maggie wanted to know why he would marry her? How could he say he wanted to live with her for the rest of his natural life? Why would she believe him? There was no way that she would. How could he convince her this was a real proposal?

So he replied quite poignantly, "Because I didn't wear a condom. You could already be pregnant." His emotion made his throat clack.

She smiled a bit and told him, "I just finished, uh, my period?" It seemed a very personal thing to mention—periods—but so was sharing sex! How much more personal could a couple get after they'd... coupled?

He was very serious as he told her earnestly, "I had some trucker friends who did it *during* her period and they still got pregnant."

Her face was quite red. "I have never been involved...in such an intimate...conversation with any man. I have all sorts of questions I'd like to ask you since you're so open. And it would be very kind if you'd let me look at you. Uh, intimately."

He gasped.

She glanced at his face and then looked seriously at him. "Would you mind? I won't hurt you. Just relax. I'm so curious to really see how it works."

He said, "Now..." He breathed oddly and he was very serious. He said, "We've already..."

"I'll be careful. You must be very tender after doing it...twice!"

He'd been thinking of her discomfort. He suggested, "We'll 'play doctor' tonight."

"Oh." She was disappointed.

"Let's get dressed and go see if we can get a license." He kissed her hands and then her mouth very sweetly.

"I have one."

That rattled him. "A *marriage* license?"

"No, no, a driver's license. We don't need a marriage license."

"We do to get married."

"Now, Ruff, we don't know each other at all well. We might not rub together well. Okay, okay." She laughed. "That way, we do, but how can we know if we can be together otherwise?"

"We'll just meet now and then and hop into bed?"

She agreed! "We'll try that first."

"Miss Donner, you shock me."

"I can't see how. I'm already so shocked over my conduct that I can't see how it could get worse."

"You're a closet prude?"

She shrugged and smiled in astonishment. "You know me better than any other man."

"Well. Physically. Yeah."

She cautioned, "You need to know me—otherwise."

"In these last two days, I've seen your reactions to all kinds of things. You're levelheaded and you adjust. Even if you're not pregnant, I want you permanent."

Soberly, Maggie replied, "We don't know each other well enough to take such a serious step."

"We've already taken a very serious one. We've just done the most intimate thing a man and a woman can do together."

She tilted her head. "Let me guess—you've married all the women with whom you've had sex?"

Ruff sighed elaborately. Who would ever believe he'd have to argue a woman into getting married?

Then she said logically, "Let's think about it." That would give them breathing room.

But he replied softly, "I have."

She grinned. "Sure." She would never forget him. How would she refer to him? Her First Lover?

Her...Highway Encounter? She regarded him fondly. However she labeled him, it would have to be in caps.

She told him, "I'm starved. Do they serve breakfast here?" She knew full well they would, but it was a nudge to get the day started ... differently. She was hungry. And it amused her to think this time it wasn't for his body but for food.

They dressed. He watched her. He had to interrupt her progress now and again. "It'll be out of sight," he complained. "I'll have only my imagination and I'm just checking to be sure I remember right."

She was new to all the old, tried-and-true bantering. She thought he was immensely clever tongued.

As they walked over to the store, the stranded truck drivers stood silently and watched the pair walk across the compound. When the pair went inside the store, those inside became silent. And they were the subject of further observation.

Ruff told her, "They're watching you."

She countered, "They're bored and would watch a rat eat."

Ruff said, "They still can't believe you're real."

She dismissed the flattery. "Naw. They're wondering how you've managed to survive the night."

He faltered just a tad and explained sotto voiced, "It wasn't easy."

And the very idea of him being imposed upon or fragile made her laugh.

* * *

The ladies' room was still sparkling clean. That rather surprised Maggie. She washed her hands and even found that a new stack of paper towels had been added to the counter.

She went out to the dining section to have breakfast. Ruff rose to seat her, and that surprised her. He hadn't seemed the type to publicly care for a woman in a place so basic.

She settled in her chair and picked up the menu.

Ruff said, "I've already ordered for you."

"You didn't have to do that." Then she asked cautiously, "What did you order?"

"The limit. I saw how you shoveled it in last night, so I was prepared to order for you this morning."

She said, "Uh-oh."

"You don't trust me." He wilted a little, as much as a man built like he could ham it up.

So she knew he was kidding . . . until she was served ham and eggs with fried potatoes, sweet rolls, coffee, milk and a bowl of cereal. There was a side dish of fruit. She looked at it all, then she looked over at him.

He was involved with his own plate and without a care. He glanced at her, saw her expression and had the audacity to inquire seriously, "What did I forget?"

Under those circumstances, she replied, "Nothing. However, I do drink tea."

"I'll take the coffee."

"How kind." She handed him the cup as she moved the ham and eggs with fried potatoes over beside his plate as one would a side dish. With relish, she ate the cereal and fruit.

He fetched her tea, which caused any amount of conversation among the other, observing truckers. "Still on the honeymoon." "They're *not!*" "That explains it." And other things said were unprintable.

Ruff suggested, "Don't listen."

She lifted interested eyes and inquired, "To what?"

"To the ravening horde?"

She tilted her head in a single nod salute. "Excellent aligning."

"You're something to watch," he told her tenderly.

She scoffed and explained the watchers. "They're bored out of their gourds."

Ruff's eyes sparkled. "I've never before heard a woman deny she was worth watching."

"Honey." She was a little elaborate in such a minutely subtle manner. "You have no idea how bored men can be. If you think I'm of primary interest, go out and move your tractor, and they'll all watch you instead."

Ruff laughed in closemouthed tolerance. "How do you know that?"

"Anyone who comes into church late is watched by bored eyes that rarely register who came in or what they wore. It's just that eyes look at anything that moves. It's done automatically."

"I believe I'm in love with you."

She nodded in agreement as she explained, "The same premise applies to men who travel alone. They are not only alone, they have time to think and they want to communicate their remarkable thoughts. Men like to talk. They need someone to talk to. Not another man. He also needs to talk and may outtalk the talker! So what a man needs is a woman who'll listen.''

''Now how did you figure all that out?''

She preened just a bit and lifted her eyebrows as she modestly looked down. Then she supplied the reply. She told him gently, ''I also travel.''

He guessed rather elaborately, ''You want to... talk!''

''Good grief.'' She was disgusted and looked around and out of the windows onto the great truck area as she waited for him to quit laughing.

Finally her eyes looked at him and they were filled with dancing lights of humor. Those emerald colors had sparkles of yellow and green and even some blue.

And again, he recognized how special she was. It scared him. She was a jewel. How could he find a jewel on the highway and damn near run her over and have her turn out this way? Did he really have the guardian angel his mother had claimed? How had this happened?

So he was quiet, and he glanced at her often to be sure she was real. And convinced that she was, he was scared.

A limping truck drove into the compound and all the idle men got up and went to the windows to watch.

She nudged him, looked at and nodded at the change and lifted her eyebrows. ''See?''

''Now you get up and we'll just see what they do.''

She deliberately scraped her chair back for the sound, and she stood up. Nobody noticed. She smothered laughter and sat back down. "Are you convinced?"

"They think you're settled here, and they can get back to looking at you."

"Oh, for Pete's sake!"

He put his hand on his stomach and said, "Having eaten two breakfasts, I can hardly move. I probably won't be able to get behind the wheel to—"

She immediately volunteered, "I'll drive!"

"No." This reply was emphatic.

"You're not only weird, you're selfish."

And with all the other drivers over at the window, still watching outside, Ruff said to her, "I've shared my body with you twice already."

She blushed scarlet and said a stern, *"Shhhh."*

"Don't you want them to know?"

"My word." She put her hand to her forehead.

While she paid the bill with her credit card, Ruff was looking into the racks and called her attention to the rings. They were glittering and had adjustable bands.

He told Maggie, "You need an engagement ring, since we've been . . . engaged." He looked at her to be sure she caught his play on words.

She considered. She squinted and licked her lips. Then she chewed on the side of her lip. "I suppose so. But it seems so blatant. I hop into bed with you and presto! I'm engaged?"

"While I do admit that's a little like backing into the room, the ring is good for appearances. Other people will realize it's not casual."

She went into another spasm of silent laughter. An adjustable ring of glass would smooth an affair? Okay.

She said, "I prefer purple."

He was shocked. "White for a virgin."

"I'm not."

"You were then."

"Virginity is like anything else. Once it's gone, it's too late to claim it. Or brag about it."

He guessed, "You want an affidavit to the fact that up until last night you were one?"

"Well, no."

"So?"

"I don't want a white glass ring. I want a purple one for passion."

"Wow!"

She looked innocent and serious. "Yes."

And he hugged her. That was such a surprise happening in that place that no one noticed.

She got the smaller, sparkling, purple glass ring; and he paid for it. He insisted. He put it on her finger and perfectly squeezed the adjustable size to fit her finger.

Her affair was legitimate.

The TV said: *This cold is unusual. Look out for neighbors. Dress in layers. Cover your nose and eyes.*

In some areas there is electrical brownout because heating is such a problem and is using so much of the resource.

Water power is not always good because mains have burst. With the ground frozen so deeply, there is no bounce or give in the ground and traffic makes the ground reverberate and rattles the mains.

Fires are horrific to control because of frozen fire hydrants and ice forming on the hoses.

Listeners were cautioned to use Vaseline on skin before covering the face.

And they showed two Chicago men with an anchored blanket tent against the wind out on the lake ice-fishing. It was too cold to fix cars that wouldn't run in that weather, but they could fish. They grinned tolerantly at the cameraperson, and they allowed him to film the nice fish catch. The lake ice was nineteen inches thick.

People in Washington, DC, were told to stay home. They were warned to have food and blankets in cars. If it was minus twelve, with the windchill it was minus fifty-three. Minus twenty was dangerously cold. And the listeners were told to keep socks and shoes dry. And if skin tingled and was white, it was frozen, and they should warm it slowly.

It was a serious storm. Even in Indiana.

6

In the truck compound café, the television was behind the counter. While the screen was big enough that everyone could see it, the TV was kept there so that George could decide the station. The fact was that the clientele never wanted to watch the same station, and the resultant constant switching had irritated the proprietor.

Since George knew everything going on in his building, he watched the selection of the purple ring. He said to Ruff, "I got better rings. I get 'em cheap. Uh, wholesale."

The old fox. Maggie smiled her Daughters of the Alamo benediction on the foxy old man and replied, "I like this one."

George didn't believe her.

And, apparently, neither did Ruff.

But she did rent a cottage for that night.

As they left the building, Ruff told her, "The white ring wouldn't've looked so cheap."

"I'm very fond of purple. White is rather boring." She glanced up at him tellingly before she added,

"Virginal." And her face was deliberately, confidingly open and precious.

Ruff sighed with forbearance as he studied his immediate area, as men do, and rubbed his chest to show it was there and he was well made and capable of anything. He mentioned, "I find you unsettle me a little."

"Well, that follows since you certainly boggle me."

He glanced at her to be sure she would understand his restraint. "I waited two days."

She half closed her eyes and looked over at him in a wasted effort. He was again seeing what was going on around his area. So she enunciated, "You waited two days because I had two decks of playing cards."

"I've been meaning to ask you about that. Why did you have those car... Oh, yeah, your sister's kids."

She informed him with the patient calm of a complete adult. "I also have a flashlight from the circus. It has a tiny elephant on top of the round bulb and when you shake the light, the sparkles reflect all over the darkened room."

"We'll do that tonight when we play doctor."

She went scarlet. She said, "Hush!"

He exclaimed in soft indignation, "It was your idea!"

"How rude of you to mention that."

And he knew that he loved her.

With most of the trucks long gone, the fax machine was idle. Maggie sent more of her pictures to her boss with the message that she would call that night or at noon their time.

Immediately, she got a return fax that the pictures were perfect. Everyone was excited about them. A film crew would land in Indy at eleven that morning and could Maggie pick them up?

She replied, "Car wrecked. Hire two cars and come north to George's truck stop."

It was Ruff who added which highways to take from the airport to the truck stop. That fax would be given to the crew when they landed in Indianapolis.

She looked up at Ruff, and he returned her regard quite seriously. She said the obvious. "They'll be here today."

"And tonight?"

She shook her head slightly as she mourned, "I must be more circumspect. They will gossip. There are some on our staff who would be—more aggressive."

He moved slightly in anguish and his eyelashes narrowed in his pain. "I understand."

"They'll only be here for a couple of days. They'll bring me a car, and I will be free to leave. I don't have to stay for the filming."

"Let them take the car back. Can you go with me when I leave?"

"No. I must go on another hunt."

"Where?"

"Along down the East Coast."

"What're'ya to look for there?"

She smiled with some nostalgia. "Actually, truck stops."

"No!" But it wasn't surprise or denial, it was shock. "I don't want you asking a bunch of truckers questions. They'll have different answers."

She lifted logical hands outward. "I can handle it."

"You only think you can."

"We have about three hours. Is there anything more that I should see?"

He replied, "Come with me. Let's get away from here."

They went out into the countryside, and she did take some pictures. She did log them. They went over the other places, and he showed her exactly how the crew could connect from one place to another.

But he backed the tractor into a farmer's field access that was screened with trees' bare branches, and he made love to her. It was sweet and poignant. It was goodbye.

He told her, "I'll be in touch. I need your fax number."

Very seriously, she replied, "It's wherever I am."

"Aren't you ever home?"

And she said sadly, "Now and then. Too rarely."

He promised, "I'll find you."

Under the sheepskin coat, lying naked against his naked body, she smoothed the hair on his head and turned little curls in that obedient mass. She smoothed the hair on his chest and loved the hairy feel of him against her own flesh.

She really understood that men's bodies are so marvelously different. While she slid her hands over his muscles with great appreciation, she didn't have the courage to really examine his sex as she wanted. It would be too personal to do before they left each other...too soon. They would part that very next day.

She asked, "When will you be through with this run? Do you have a place I can get in touch with you?"

He took out a book and read from it. All the places were lined up. Drop here, pick up there, go on to that place. He copied it all down with the phone numbers. Nothing was anywhere near to where she'd be. She had no real places or phone numbers to give him.

That panicked him. She could slip away forever. The one number of her business base was especially iffy. She identified the place as an understaffed madhouse.

She told him, "Basically, they're all artists. Photographers are. While they aren't of the fine arts, their attitude is similar. They tend to disregard anything but light, angle and color."

Then, gently, she told him, "This has been a miracle time. I will always value knowing you. No, don't interrupt. Let me tell you. You're special. You are such a man. I'm glad the world has you. You care about people, and you help automatically. You're skilled as a truck driver, you're a compassionate rescuer and you're a wonderful lover. I'm glad you were my first to—"

He interrupted somewhat stridently. "First! How many do you plan on using?"

Very sweetly she replied, "I didn't use you!"

Angrily he asked, "What's all this talk about me being your 'first' lover!"

"You were!"

And again he asked, "How many more do you plan on taking?"

She was a trifle more formal. "I didn't 'take' you. We made love."

He closed his eyes and breathed to calm himself. Then he said with great intensity, "I don't want to lose you."

"You won't."

"I don't feel this is solid. I think it's a fluke. I'm afraid I'll only get to dream about you for the rest of my life."

"I'm not that important to you. We've only known each other three days."

He was emphatic. "Three days is long enough. We've been together all that time. It would be like being with you for three hours at a time and that would add up to—knowing each other for twenty-six consecutive days. Anybody knowing somebody else for almost a month, knows them."

She agreed, "You know me more—intimately— than anyone else does."

"We have to have a meeting soon. We need to plan it so that I don't go crazy wondering where you are. Where do you go after the East Coast?"

She hugged him and rubbed her face into his naked shoulder. He felt the tears. His voice gravelly, he told her, "If you cry, you'll ruin me."

Tightly, she denied it. "I'm not crying."

He leaned back slowly and lifted his hand to tilt up her chin so that he could look at her face. Her lashes were wet but she ignored that as she returned his stare.

His tone roughened, he said, "I've got a really bad case of you."

"We met under dramatic circumstances." She explained it all. "With the wreck, your attention was pulled to me. You feel responsible for me because you knew you had ruined my car. This is mostly a guilt trip. When I get another car, it will release you from this trap."

"You're the trap. You move just right. Your humor is just right. You kiss just right. You are sassy and brave and you like me and babies. You let me make love. And you haven't whined or used it as a hammer on me."

"Had many of those?"

That either annoyed him or it hit a nerve for he said instantly, "Cut it out. I'm in shock and I'm scared I might not find you again."

She shrugged wonderfully and her naked breast moved in a brush against the surface of his hairy chest. So he didn't immediately hear what she said and she had to repeat the words. She'd said, "I would find you. I have a friend in Chicago who locates people. She's a Lambert from TEXAS. She would find you."

"Lambert?"

"Yes. Hillary Lambert Behr."

Ruff mused with memories. "I've heard of the family. Her dad rides, uh, ornery mules?"

"That's the one."

"We call them stubborn—TEXANS call them ornery."

"I know," she replied.

"When have you *ever* had to handle a mule?"

"I've heard tell of the actual mule, but I've contended with the male variety quite a lot. Men tend to be both stubborn *and* ornery."

He said stridently, "I've never been either!"

But she shot down his balloon by saying darkly, "Not yet."

"Now, why would you believe that I'd be difficult?"

"Your hard, short, stubby thumbs."

"So?"

"Your clenched fist is like a mallet."

His lower lip out a way, his head forward, he asked, "What's that got to do with control?"

She did that distracting shrug again and replied, "You've kept it so far?"

"You think I've got a temper?"

"No. But you can become angry. Not easily. I've been a burr on you for three days, now, and I've seen remarkable control. These three hours are the twenty-eighth day."

"Did you think when I made love to you that I was gentle?"

"Yes."

"I'm glad you realize it was you that lost control. I was being so careful with you. I only wanted to dip into you and then put on the condom. You were the wild one."

"I've always been a lady."

"I've noticed."

"That doesn't sound sincere."

"I mean it from the bottom of my heart."

"Where is your heart?" She put her hand on his chest and her lashes were lowered to see there.

"Lower."

She looked up at him. "In your stomach?"

His voice husky, he told her, "The roots go lower. You'll find one of the roots down a way."

She shifted back a little and ran her hand down the silken hair on his stomach...and lower. "*Ahhh.* There it is."

And his breathing was audible.

She took him into her hand and looked back up to his face. "It's pulsing."

"It's excited."

"Why is it still excited?"

"I don't know. Let's find out."

They got back to the truck stop about ten minutes before the photo crew arrived. Linda was with the crew. "I'm the same size as the Star," she told Maggie. "She's too valuable to risk in this bitter weather. I'm her stand-in for the long shots and back shots. If I catch pneumonia, Fred told the crew to drag me along or prop me up but pull the hat down and turn up my collar. And I don't have to go barefooted, I can wear boots. A perk."

Maggie shook her head in awe. "You get to do all that? Golly, I'll bet she's so jealous!"

Josh asked Maggie, "Where'd you get that coat? It would be great for the film. Let us rent it."

"It's Ruff's. Ask him."

But Ruff said, "It's Maggie's."

So they dickered. They'd buy her a full-length leather coat to wear, which she could keep, and they said she'd get the sheepskin coat back, on their *honors!*

That set off a stunning round of hilarity.

But Maggie told them she couldn't and wouldn't give up the coat, and they'd just have to find another.

They groused cheerfully that she was hard-nosed and selfish.

She agreed.

Ruff watched her through his eyelashes. He didn't add any comment.

Linda asked Maggie, "Is it okay if I bunk with you?"

Maggie didn't look over at the watching Ruff. She replied softly, "Of course."

Some sadness in Maggie's voice hung in Linda's ear. Her head came up. "Got another roomie?"

"No." The word was so sadly soft.

They all went out that afternoon and just compared the places with the shots. They were exuberant. No matter how they tried to figure it, they could not use the schoolhouse, but they filmed it.

Josh told Ruff, "I understand you lost part of your truck. That explains why you're so quiet. I guess when a guy has a truck like that, it's home?"

And Ruff replied, "Yeah. Something like that."

Jon put in, "I know how you feel. Our farmhouse burned down. I was ten. At that age, life is supposed to be level. To have the house burn was trauma for me. But my parents mourned pictures, a wedding album, that kind of stuff. I mourned my room. I had a stuffed owl."

The L.A. people talked earthquakes after the 1993 teeth-rattler that had thousands of echo quakes.

Maggie said, "They seem to think that area will separate into another island. Who'd get it?"

"We annexed Hawaii with that very thing in mind. It'd be another state."

Josh pronounced, "No. We'd finally have our own country. It'd be ours!"

So, of course, TEXAS native Maggie told the rules of TEXAS joining the U.S. and the clause that said they could withdraw from the union or they could break up into five states if they so chose.

That brought on a whole lot of arguing and hoopla and snorts and laughter, which lasted through supper back at the truck compound.

All that while, it interested Ruff how Maggie rode through it all. They could not ruffle her feathers. She gave as good as she got. And she gently mentioned the fact that Band-Aids wouldn't solve California's urge to independently leave the mainland the way that California terrain had recently been indicating it would like to do.

They were a good group.

* * *

When the others had gone to bed, only Maggie and Ruff were still at the table. But they were hardly alone. They were under the checking gazes of other truckers who were newly arrived, eating, visiting together and curious about the silent couple.

Maggie was asked to dance by just about every man there. Unusually, there were no other women, and Linda had gone to bed. Maggie declined each one. "I have to talk to Ruff."

But the two had little to say.

In the turmoil of laughter, country music and foot-stomping dancing, the lovers were silent; their eyes met to cling, to tear apart and then meet again.

She said, "I'm going to miss you."

The words would have been okay, but her eyes were as big as saucers, and her lower lip trembled with finishing the word "you."

He groaned.

"Don't."

"Don't...what?"

"Don't groan." She dipped a hand as if at a fly by her chin. "You're making me miserable."

He cast her a disgruntled glance. "No other woman has ever ruined me like you have in this short time that—"

"Short? You've told me quite earnestly that we've known each other for almost a month!" She was a little indignant.

His eyelashes covered his eyes as he looked down. He said one word to correct her tabulation, "Years."

This time it was her voice that trembled. "It seems so, doesn't it. There is so much for me to remember. How can you leave me?"

That made him indignant. "It's you leaving me! And you called in all those dogs who're barking and howling—"

"They are not!"

His voice was soft. "I know." He looked up at her, and she could actually see into his blue eyes. He told her, "I'm miserable, too. I want you to just be with me. I'm jealous that they can treat you like friends."

"Remember that's all they are."

"I have proof."

Her cheeks pinkened but she told him, "You're wonderful."

"I'm scared you're gonna find a guy who's better and smoother."

She shook her head. "I don't see how."

"Don't look."

"I won't."

He promised, "I won't, either. But how can I be sure you won't forget me next week."

"I have my ring."

He looked at the purple glass ring. "Wear it until I can get you a good one."

"I shall."

Just the fact that she'd replied with a word like "shall" shivered his timbers. They were too different. And he finally realized he would lose her. She would get away from him to somebody with normal parents who named their kids Tom and Dick and

Harry. Someone who would have a son who would catch her eye. He'd be better than a silly tractor driver called Ruffan Reddy.

Ruff decided he would tell his dad what a disaster his labeling name had been.

And he knew he couldn't do that to his dad. The name was just something he'd have to live with for the rest of his life. That, and the loss of Maggie Donner.

It was a terrible thing to sit in a chair at a table, looking at her, and know he was losing a woman like her. There was not one damned thing he could do about it. Out of sight, he would be out of her mind. Gone.

He took her to her cabin and kissed her good-night. It was really goodbye. He would be leaving the next day. There would be no other time that he could hold her as he wanted, and kiss her as he wanted. This was it. The end.

She leaned against him and held him and she rubbed her face against his throat. She still wore the sheepskin and was warm.

It was his sheepskin coat that kept her warm. How could that be so important to him? It was.

He released her gently, and he said, "I'll find you."

She looked at him, puzzled. Find her? She wasn't lost. Or— Was she? She realized then that was how she felt. Lost. Adrift. The tears began to slide down her cheeks without her permission.

And in the glint of the night lights, Ruff saw the tears. That tore his heart in two just as it filled his whole being. She would cry because he had to leave her? To part from her? Maybe there was hope?

He groaned so softly and took her against him yet again. "Ah, Maggie, my heart."

They stood there clasped together until he finally realized nothing good could come of such misery. They had to let go. He needed to get to bed and sleep if he was to drive tomorrow. He released her slowly. He kissed her sweetly, softly, a salute.

He told her, "I'll be in touch."

"Yes."

"I'll be leaving early. You need the sleep. Don't get up. It'll be tough enough to leave here without you coming to say goodbye to me again. We've said it and it just stretches out and hurts us both."

That's what he said. It was logical. She hugged him with all her strength. Then she had to let go of him. Then she had to indicate that he was supposed to let go of her. And gradually, reluctantly, slowly he began to let her go.

She stood there.

So did he.

Her lower lip trembled.

He took her back into his arms and held her as he shook his head against the side of hers and he made soft, pain-filled sounds.

It was awful.

Maggie finally softly went inside the cabin, taking great pains so as not to waken Linda. Linda did waken and was silent. No one could be half cognizant and not hear the almost silent nose blowing, the open-mouthed, shivering breaths and the faint sighs. Maggie was being so stealthy and quiet that Linda knew she didn't want anyone to realize she loved that trucker, Ruffan Reddy. What a name.

But at dawn, there Maggie was, standing in the window with the drape held back, looking outside where Reddy's big tractor was moving. The sound came closer, closer and it stopped by their cabin.

It was so noisy that Linda hadn't at first realized Maggie had rushed to the door, thrown it open and run outside.

Linda roused up and watched against the headlights. She saw Maggie throw herself against Ruff, and they stood locked together.

Oh, dear.

Then Ruff picked Maggie up and carried her back to the cabin and set her on her feet in the doorway. And their kiss made Linda decide that she didn't love Murray enough to become that serious with him.

Linda then covered her head and left the couple some privacy.

It was a while before Linda heard the truck's motor pick up again and the sound came a little closer before it began slowly to go away.

It was a while after that before the door to the cabin closed and Maggie went back to the other bed—and the muffled tears started again.

Really, Linda thought, why the problem? The solution was simple. She should have just gone with the guy. What was more important?

7

The film crew didn't need Maggie around. They had Linda there as a substitute for the leading lady. They had Ruff's good direction on where to find what. Maggie could leave. They'd brought her the rental car. She was free.

She lingered. She dragged around. She sat and listened as they plotted out when they'd film what where. The sun did not show its face. They thought that was good. No shadows. They put that down.

And after lunch they went out, telling Maggie, "Take care of yourself." "Drive safely." "It's been good to see you again." And they said they'd be intensely interested in her research down in a *better climate!*

The four left.

Maggie was alone.

She packed. She sat and stared into space. She went to George's store and had a glass of milk. She opened one of the books. But she was so taken into the trials of the hero and heroine that she had to put the book aside until she was stronger and a bit less empathetic.

Misery.

Self-pity.

She took her camera and her one bag to the rental car with her granddaddy's blanket and what was left of the granola bars. She refilled the thermos and put it all into the car. It was mud colored. She really didn't notice what it looked like.

She went to the office part of the main building. There she found that Ruff had paid for her room. That made her even more vulnerable, so she went to the café part of the building and had a cup of tea.

Finally, finally, she left. She drove away in the ugly rental car rather sour-mouthed because it wasn't her own little white car.

She learned more about different driving with the rental as she went along. It had its own flaws and was obstinate about little things. Driving such a cranky car did distract her.

So then she wondered if car rental people deliberately put quirks into their cars so that the renters would pay attention to their driving? It would be a wreck deterrent.

That led her into thinking how interestingly people thought. Minds were crafty and clever. All sorts of subtle means were used to catch others' attention. People were subtle.

Well. Not her acquaintance, Phyl. She was different. Phyl would lie back on the sofa with her eyes closed. Her head would roll in exquisite agony as she'd slowly rub both her hands down from under her breasts to her thighs and slowly back up her hips as she'd groan, "Just the *word* penetration..."

How strange to suddenly be empathetic with Phyl!

Several days passed. It took some driving before there was a significant change in the weather. It was hard to find a motel room with any vacancies. People were staying put rather than struggling with the weather.

Maggie watched Ruff's list and knew where he was. His truck would get through. She could call him. What would she say?

She had to hear his voice. But it wasn't until about three nights after that before she did call him.

He asked immediately, "Where are you?"

"In Knoxville."

"How was the road?"

"Interesting."

"We had a hell of a time on out in Watertown. That's in South Dakota."

"Did you find a place to stay over?"

"There're truck stops along the way just like over off I-69 in Indiana."

"I saw a truck tractor like yours."

"You didn't wink at the guy, did you?"

"No. But I looked at the tractor quite enviously."

"Because you thought I was in it?"

"Well, actually, I figured it would be warmer than the car I had."

"Don't get in tractor cabs with strangers."

"I know. It's dangerous."

There was some silence before he asked softly, "Do you think I'm . . . dangerous?"

"Very."

"Not around you. I'm very careful."

She smiled into the phone, but he only heard her silence. Then there was the soft click as she hung up.

He hung up his own phone softly. He was serious. She'd been a virgin. Did she now regret the fact that a stranger from nowhere, a traveling man, had been her first? Would he ever again hear from her? So he sweat until she called him the next time.

When Maggie called, Ruff actually shivered when he heard her voice on the phone. He hadn't known how intensely he'd waited to hear from her. Or how much he worried whether or not she would call again.

So he was prosaic. "Where're you?"

She replied without any feeling of being a miracle at all, and she said quite simply, "In Polk City, Florida."

"Where in Florida is that?"

"From top to bottom and side to side, it's just about exactly in the middle. They have a single traffic light that is a yellow flasher in the middle of a block. There's a road outside it called Holy Cow. I'm not sure that's for the Cubs' play announcer Harry Caray, but for him that sign must have a familiar ring.

"They've taken a film of me standing there holding on a big hat against the wind so the star can be there waiting for someone to come off the connecting highway to pick her up. No one but Harry Caray devotees will see the sign. They don't do anything to call attention to it other than having the 'heroine' standing there briefly. They go to great lengths to be droll."

Ruff didn't really want to talk about the filming. But he told her, "I'll get a copy of the movie just to resee that section until I have it worn-out and have to copy it five or six times."

"Everyone will assume you're a Harry Caray fan."

"Not when they notice you."

She laughed softly in his ear.

He told her with his mouth close to the mouthpiece, "It's cold up here."

In some surprise, Maggie replied, "I thought you were made for that kind of northern climate."

"I've been burned by such a hot woman that I can't stand the cold anymore."

"Balderdash."

"Balder-dash?" He tasted the word.

"It's very similar to baloney."

He gave up on the chatter and asked the serious question, "When can I see you?"

"I've noticed that you'll be in Illinois in four weeks? I'll be in St. Louis."

"I'll figure a way."

And she said, "I'd need somebody to take me around the area. Somebody with a truck cab for rent?"

He corrected, "Tractor cab." Then he added with droll concern, "I'll see what I can do about that."

"I have you listed in Champaign-Urbana in twenty-four days with a side trip to Vandalia before a turn-around?"

"Yeah."

"How long can you lay over?"

He choked and coughed in a fake way. "All the time you've got. I'll quit trucking for any length of time you got open."

She asked carefully, "Are you paying alimony to anybody?"

"I've never been married. I told you that."

She explained, "I believe you said you weren't married. You could have once been. I'd hate for any little kids to starve while you're lounging around on the Mississippi."

"No problem." Then he asked with interest, "We're going on a boat ride?"

"We just might."

He was comfortable talking on her quarter. In a visiting manner, he went on, "I was in St. Louis during the 1993 flood, and the river looked just fine. A very fast current in midstream that'd make you squint your eyes, but the bushes were above water and the boats were moored along the shore. Then I found out the bushes were *treetops* and the boats were moored over the parking lots!"

"What were you doing there?"

"We hauled in sandbags."

She bragged on him, "The sandbags saved the town."

"No. It was the dam. The sandbags leaked, and the river went over and through and under them. Did you see the pictures of the baseball stadium with the ducks swimming along first base?"

"Yes! In Dubuque!"

"It was interesting to see along the area, how people took the flood. They were foolish to've built there, but they were—noble."

"They were."

Then he asked, "What are you driving? A rental?"

"No, I bought a new car. Red."

His voice turned a little husky. "I can't wait to see you."

"Next week, I'll call you at Colorado Springs?"

"Yeah." His voice in her ear was soft and tender. Then he sighed. Finally he said, "About St. Louis, you got reservations yet?"

"At Adam's Mark. I have a meeting at the hotel."

"Good. I can leave a message there if I have to. I mean to be there. Be careful driving and don't flirt with any truckers."

"I never did, until just recently."

"Nobody else is like me. You've already gotten the best there is. Call me in Colorado Springs."

"If I can."

Ruff's voice become more roughened. "Wherever you are, call me."

Her words tangled. "I...I'm looking forward... Well, I will be glad to see you again."

"Me, too."

In an earnest little voice, Maggie asked him seriously, "Are you really like I think of you?"

His voice blurred a trifle. "How do you think of me?"

"King of the road?"

His voice was speculative. "Maybe one of the dukes?"

"I'll check you out."

"All right!"

So Maggie's phone bills were mounting. Ruff tried to pay her back. He'd say to send him the bills. She replied, "It was my call."

"But you know where I am. I never know where you are." Then reluctantly he admitted, "I'm afraid I could lose you."

"I tell you where I am."

He chided, "Only when you call. Otherwise I don't have you in a place. I don't know if you're in a car or a motel or hotel or if some guy's hassling you."

"I know judo."

"My God! You shoulda told me that right away when my tractor hit your car! You coulda flipped me."

"Chopped," she corrected in a kind voice.

"If I'd known, I would have been scared and behaved more politely."

Her voice smiled as she replied, "I'm glad you didn't know."

"You shameless huzzzzy!" And the word carried the *z*'s.

But she only responded in a nice intimate purr, "I'm looking forward to seeing you again."

"I'm forward, thinking about you."

"How shocking."

"You will be." His breaths had picked up. "I've missed you something awful. I think of you a whole lot. My cab is empty."

"Keep it that way."

He laughed as he groaned.

In those next weeks, Maggie talked to Ruff in several places. When he was in Casper, she was in Arizona. It had been a long three weeks for Ruff. He could hardly wait past their greeting before he asked, "You okay?"

"Fine. Are you all right?"

"It's been some weeks since—we were together. Are you okay?"

"Oh, you mean . . . yes. I'm fine. This week. We didn't . . . I'm okay."

"Darn."

That made her laugh the softest, most charming way he'd ever heard.

As usual they talked on the phone as they would have over a backyard fence. They were getting acquainted. They told what was going on and why they were where they were.

He told her the cleaner jokes he'd heard. And he loved her laugh in his ear.

With his voice husky and licking his lips in audible sounds in her ear, he said more than once, "I can't wait to see you again."

Reluctantly, she told him. "In St. Louis, I'll be sharing a room with a woman I know. This came about in a strange and baffling way. She insisted she needed an outing. I had mentioned St. Louis, and all of a sudden I have a roomie. I didn't know how to tell her I didn't want her along."

"Is she single."

"Yes."

"How old?"

"My age. I knew her rather remotely at school, and she's always rather startled me."

"I'll find a guy for her."

"Uh, I'm not sure I can recommend her. She might shock some men."

"I'll find one who'll shock her."

"Now, Ruff, you must know I can't allow that."

Ruff explained, "I know all types of guys. If she's a wild and woolly woman, I can find a guy to match her."

With grinding reluctance, Maggie said again, "She does startle me. I don't believe I'd want to cope with her conduct with a man of the type you mention. I'd probably freeze up."

"Well, we certainly don't want anything like that to happen!"

"Perhaps we ought to postpone our meeting until another time? I'm sure we can arrange something else."

But Ruff was positive. "No!"

Then she said, "We'll see."

So he got to sweat it. The only good thing he could see was that she would be at the Adam's Mark Hotel—if she hadn't changed hotels.

He carefully wrote a very serious letter to her and mailed it to the hotel in St. Louis to hold for her. Since they'd parted, it was the first time he'd known of a place where she would be.

And he spent a lot of restless time wondering if she'd back out of their rendezvous. Then he remembered that she had set it up because she had a meeting there. So she would have to be in St. Louis. Where? Logically, the meeting would be at that hotel. And he breathed a little easier.

Then it occurred to him that just maybe the meeting was somewhere close by, and she'd planned to keep him separate from the people she was scheduled to meet.

Yeah.

He rubbed his face with both hands and walked around the warehouse dock where the trailer was being unloaded. He generally watched. He went back to stand by and watch.

But he didn't actually see what was being done. He knew the loaders were aware of him, and they were skilled, so as he stood there, he could go back to thinking about Maggie.

How could he have gotten tangled up with a woman like Maggie?

That was the opening to a lot of deadly serious thought.

Meanwhile, by then, at home in the far, northside of San Antonio, TEXAS, Maggie was thinking about Ruff. She didn't call him from home. She wasn't sure, yet, of her feelings for him. Just because such a gorgeous man ran her car down on a snow-drifting, wind-swirling blind day on a highway in Indiana, didn't mean he was really and truly a King of the Road.

Despite the fact that he looked like a contender for a top place, he might have the morals of an alley cat. Her mother had warned her about just such a thing.

As Maggie was polishing her toenails in her room at home, her mother lounged on the bed and watched. In the next silence, her mother mentioned with perfect casualness, "You've met someone."

Maggie lifted her eyebrows in an adult manner and replied, "I'm always meeting someone. Which 'one' are you referring to?"

"The one you were thinking about when I came into the room."

"Oh. I was wondering how the team did in...east Georgia at the site I found there." Maggie then looked fully at her mother with adult patience.

Her mother's eyes closed halfway down as she asked, "Who is he?"

"Who is whom?"

"The man who has you vague and rattled and makes you smile now and then for no reason."

Maggie considered. "The film crew was in great spirits in Indiana. Linda got to substitute for the star with her back to—"

"So he's in Indiana?"

Being adult and twenty-six to boot, Maggie lifted her chin and frowned a little as she looked as if she was listening to something in the distance. "Indiana? Why... Indiana?"

"You've been several places since then, what makes you go back to Indiana for something that feeble to mention?"

"There is nothing feeble about Linda posing outside in that bitter cold. And anyway, I lost my car in Indiana."

"Who was the truck driver who took it out?"

"Some man."

"What's he look like?"

"*Ummmm.* I don't remember, exactly. Why do you want to know?"

"You're distracted. Something is bothering you."

Well, while that *was* true, Maggie didn't see any reason to spill it all to her mother. She replied, "I suppose I've been a little pushed."

"How do you like your new car? I thought it would be white, you liked the other one so much."

"The trucker said to get red. He hadn't been able to see it against the snow."

"What was he like?"

"Male. Positive. Kind. He didn't get hysterical when he shoved my car off the highway and into the snow."

"What happened then?"

"We waited to be rescued. His trailer was knocked sideways. I've mentioned this all before. What were you thinking about when I've told this same story before?"

"You're—different."

Maggie observed her mother with mature tolerance and replied, "I'm older."

"When you want to share, I'm here."

"Share? Share...what? Bonding? Recipes? Patterns? Gossip?"

"Try the gossip part." Her mother was still watching Maggie in that careful way with her eyes a little squinched.

"You already know that Phyl is going with me to St. Louis."

"Is that...gossip?"

"I don't believe you have assimilated the real Phyllis."

"What should I have seen?"

"I'm unsure of her public social conduct away from TEXAS."

Her mother opened out both hands as if exposing logic. "Don't include her on your trip."

"I didn't. She horned in."

"Her family isn't outrageous."

"You've known the family for some time, tell me about her genetic contributors."

"Unless she's a blanket child, all her kin are modest and normal."

"Maybe she was switched at the hospital?"

"She is old enough that you aren't responsible for her conduct."

"Ah, but she has chosen to accompany me. How do I wiggle out of that?"

"Cancel?"

"This meeting is important to me. It could mean a boost in my responsibility. I need to be there."

"Then be firm and truthful to Phyl. Give her limits which she must follow or she doesn't go with you. Tell her now."

"How can I tell her that when I have no positive knowledge of her conduct. She's acted like a cat on a hot tin roof on occasion, but just with women who she makes laugh at her."

"Why did you agree to her going with you?"

"She invited herself."

"Well, since she's the age she is, she is responsible for her own conduct, and you are not her keeper."

"Ah, but how far do I allow her to go when she is my guest? I believe you have used the expression Birds of a Feather? If she is publicly salacious, it will reflect on me. Right?"

"How did you allow yourself to get in this mess?"

"She just did it and ran with it."

"Next time that happens, stop it immediately. You have allowed it to happen. It is up to you to cancel her out of your plans, or put up with her conduct. It is a difficult lesson. I would advise you to cancel."

So Maggie called Phyl and said to her answering machine, "Phyl, this is Margaret Donner. I am sorry, but I can't include you on the trip to St. Louis. Perhaps next time."

The next day on the Donner answering machine was a reply from Phyl. "Hi. I loved your hilarious message! Not go? Don't be silly! Looking forward to being with you. Love ya, Phyl."

Yes.

Packing to go to Missouri, Maggie said, "Goody."

"Live and learn. After this, don't tell anyone where or how you're going."

"They ask."

"Say it's secret and your boss forbids it."

So Maggie called Phyl again and said to her answering machine, "This is Margaret Donner. Phyllis, I will not be leaving from home. I cannot take you along. My activities would not include you. Perhaps we can have lunch when I return."

And she left.

Maggie drove to Missouri, saw and walked through and talked to the inhabitants of Ste Genevieve to observe the recovery from the 1993 floods. And after that, she arrived at the Adam's Mark Hotel in St. Louis. She was dressed for the city.

The registration clerk handed her a letter and mentioned, "Your friend has already arrived."

"What—friend?" Maggie was looking at the letter from Ruff. Was he already there?"

"Miss Phyllis Allen?"

How amazing. How hardnosed of the woman to come anyway after being twice rebuffed. How could

Maggie stop Ruff from landing in that predicament and have Phyl knowing Maggie had arranged to meet him there? What a mess!

She asked, "Can I have a room alone?"

"We're filled up. I'm sorry."

"If there's a cancellation, would you save it for me?"

"I'll put you on the list."

"Is Mr. Ruff U. Reddy registered?"

"Yes."

"His room number?"

"I'll leave a message that you need to contact him."

"Will you give him my room number?"

"We'll relay his call and you can do that yourself."

"Is Miss Allen in my room?"

"I'll call." He did, but there was no response.

With her luggage, Maggie went up the elevator to the eighth floor and went to the room. It was obvious that Phyl had been there. She had taken the bed near the window and filled the top drawers and most of the hangers with her clothes. Her roomie. There was a note. *I'm on the top floor at the swimming pool. Phyl!*

It was going to be a fun couple of days, and Maggie had no one to blame but herself.

Maggie grimly unpacked and put her things away in the space left for her. She resisted pushing Phyl's things aside, even in the bathroom. She would get through this time and she would never again allow any such thing to happen. Never.

She dressed in a black utilitarian suit and had her room key in a suit pocket. She wore high heels and put Ruff's letter in her inside pocket. She could feel it against her chest. If she touched it, there was a slight crackling sound. Why a letter?

She went down and registered for her meeting. It was a conference for those who sought backgrounds for films, including those filmed for schools, for instruction for manufacturers, for orientation and incidentally for the least of the problems, for movies and TV.

Maggie's little niche was small potatoes. How strange. Everyone thinks of films as being movies, but the vast number of structured films concern just about everything else. Most of the other films are not available or of interest to the general public. The interest span was important, but limited. They were advertising, food sales, information, safety, how-to, medical procedures, that sort of thing.

TV had more representatives there than those of the movie industry. Even the TV attendees were limited. Most of the TV backgrounds were a stage or series of stages. Something familiar for the viewers.

And the people attending the gathering were assorted as always. The gender mix was mostly male.

Interested men came casually in a beeline and smiled. They stood by Maggie and inquired offhandedly, "Cereal? Cars?"

"Movies."

"Oh. That must be interesting. Where all do you go?"

"Just about everywhere. I'm seldom anyplace very long." She said that gently.

And invariably, the male would nod sagely and say, "Here's my card. If you're ever in my area, let me help."

"Thank you."

Within just an hour, she had about a dozen cards in her pocket. That was good and one reason she was there. If the film background group had a local, anywhere, the local would know the terrain and could be a big help. Just like Ruff had been off I-69 in Indiana. It was an area he knew.

Of course, it was better to have a card than to risk being shoved off a highway by a truck in order to meet a local.

8

Maggie still had Ruff's letter burning a hole in her jacket pocket. Why had he sent her...a letter? He was at the hotel. He hadn't canceled being there. She knew it. She would see him. Did the letter mean he was going to be kind and reject her in person? She didn't want to read a thick letter that was a long goodbye.

Her thinking scrambled around and hurried and wasn't exactly coherent.

Why was she so zonked? Things happened. Plans were changed in any business or friendship. Just because she'd been snowbound for several days with a man, it didn't mean they had bonded. People had all sorts of disappointments. The weather, tires flattened, shipments went wrong. There were all kinds of things.

But he was there! The letter was fat. He couldn't have written that big of an alibi just to say goodbye.

Maybe he would think she needed a long explanation if his conscience was really bugging him. After all, they'd shared some intense time, much humor, conversation...and their bodies. Yes.

He wouldn't just not contact her; he did write to her. But after all that effort, would he really come there to face her? He *was* there. How strange that he had arrived, but the long letter was postmarked over two weeks ago.

Did he feel he had to be present to discard her? That didn't add up. Why would he have changed his mind? What in the world was going on?

With part of her mind off wandering around, arguing and debating, Maggie seemed serene and courteous and somewhat mysterious. She smiled and nodded and replied and remembered. She appeared somewhat aloof. She was especially good at names.

Since she wasn't pawing or holding on to any of the willing males, some of the women came over and joined her in conversation. They were charming and very sharp minded. The humor and quickness was stimulating. Maggie gladly put their cards in her pocket also.

The day went by at the accelerated speed of any well-done seminar.

Just about everyone was including and open. Maggie was asked any number of times to join someone or a group for dinner. And she declined. She still needed to read the letter.

She heard one of the women gasp and say, "Will you look at that!"

Maggie didn't recognize him at first. He was in a dark suit, white shirt and red tie. He stood, perfectly at ease, and he looked around without stretching up or making a show of it.

She hadn't read the letter.

People—mostly women—went up and questioned him. He smiled a little and said something brief and continued to look—for her. He was looking for her. Why?

How dare he come looking for her, to discard her, looking like that? He looked like every woman's dream of a man. But she knew he could look that way in grease-covered coveralls or nothing at all. And Maggie's bones melted and her lower stomach yearned in a very unladylike manner.

She stood still, watching him, and she saw him as his searching eyes found her. He grinned, then he looked down her and back up as he came to her. He never took his eyes from her.

The women around Maggie took in little gasps of air as he came to that group. And the men minutely jerked or moved in territorial attitudes. Men would do that with Ruff around.

But Ruff didn't pay any attention. He just came to the group, put out a hand to take hold of Maggie's elbow and he said, "Excuse us."

Well, if he was going to be a gentleman about it, she might just as well hear what he had to say. She smiled at the group and said for herself, "Excuse me."

She allowed him to take her elbow in his hand, and she walked out with him. She glanced at him, and his eyes were filled with delight, and he licked his smile like a tomcat. What was in that letter?

His hand slid down her arm and held her hand. His fingers sought her ring finger. The purple ring was there! Lifting her hand to kiss the ring, he said, "You got here! It took years, but we finally got together again. Did they give you my letter?"

"I haven't had time to read it, yet."

"Read it after you leave me. It's good for anytime. I need all your attention."

That didn't sound like any rejection.

"Have you missed me?" He grinned at her, confident of her reply.

Her honest, independent mouth replied, "Yes."

"You haven't thrown your arms around me and kissed me, yet, as you rub your body—" He stopped and looked around the empty hall. "Quick, there's nobody right now." And he kissed her.

It was simply stupendous. How'd he learn to kiss like that?

As he lifted his mouth from hers and looked at her very seriously, and a tad blurred, she asked, "Where did you learn to kiss thataway?"

"I practiced on my hand."

Laughter bubbled up and her eyes began to dance as she returned his regard. "I've missed you."

He hugged her tightly and shivered. "Oh, Maggie, my heart." Then he asked seriously, "Is this real or was it just propinquity?"

Maggie chided, "I know what that there word means! You showing off?"

"I told you my mother was a stickler." But he then answered her question. "We'd be this way no matter how we'd met or for how long. I recognized you as soon as I got your car door opened. How soon was it for you?"

"I'm still a little rattled."

"Rattled?" He squeezed her against him, still standing there in the hall, keeping them both upright while the people passed them—

There were other people in the hall! She sobered and looked around and stiffened a little and stood more firmly on her own feet.

One of the men whose card was in her pocket commented, "*Ahh.* Now I understand."

She thought fleetingly that he must have an impressive seduction record.

But after he passed them, she took the cards from her pocket and shuffled through until she found his, and she slid it into Ruff's suit pocket.

Ruff guessed, "You thought he was a business contact?"

"Actually, yes."

"Ah, you might just as well pitch all the others."

"No. Some are okay. And actually, he would be also. You ruined the contact by hugging and kissing me so outrageously here in public, this way. He'll think I just met you and I'm easy. But I get cards from people at places like this because they would know what backgrounds in their district we might need. They know their area like you know your truck routes. I don't just go out, driving around, waiting for a miracle to jump from behind the bushes saying 'Voilà!'"

"I opened your car door and there you were."

"I believe you ought to loosen your arms a little. People are staring."

"It's okay. We'll probably never see them again."

"I have some of their cards. I need to conduct myself more conservatively." She looked up at him very seriously. Then she added, "—in public."

His eyes began to sparkle, and he bit into his lower lip as he loosened his arms one millimeter.

She suggested, "A tad more."

So they went on down the scale of loosening, quite slowly.

By then, the people at the meeting had all departed and the couple was alone. He took advantage of that and kissed her witless.

Then he foolishly asked her questions. "Did you bring that woman along?"

Each question took a while for Maggie to sort through the purple haze and find a reply. She finally told him, "I declined to bring her here—"

"Well, Terry can find—"

"But she came, anyway. She was swimming on the top floor. In the pool up there."

"We can go—"

"She'll have come down by now and dressed for dinner. Her clothes are in my room."

"You shouldn't have unpacked. We'll move you over to mine."

"I can't do that."

"Well, some of them? Just you? No change of clothing? You'll sleep naked?" He went back to hugging her too closely.

"You're stronger than you realize."

He leaned his head back. "Why?"

"You're squashing me."

His arms immediately loosened. "Did I *hurt* you?" He was appalled.

"No. But you limit my breathing."

He understood and shared the knowledge, "You louse mine up."

"How could I possibly?"

"Looking at you makes me pant. Talking to you on the phone makes me just about suffocate. But I hold you like this and everything gets out of hand." He grinned down at her. "Want to feel around and see the difference?"

With her body stretched up along his, she laughed as she blushed and slid one hand from his shoulder to cover her face.

"It's time to meet Terry and introduce him to— what was her name?"

"Phyllis Allen."

"Yeah. Terry's curious."

"Is he a truck driver, too?"

"More like a dispatcher."

And uncomfortably, Maggie felt the need to warn Ruff. "I didn't invite her. She can be pushy. Can he handle a pushy woman?"

"He likes that kind best."

After some agonized movements of her mouth and a variety of frowns, Maggie was finally forced to warn Ruff, "Terry might never be able to get rid of her. I declined having her along, twice."

"We'll see what happens. He's a grown man, and he's not easily led."

So Maggie narrowed her eyes and asked, "Where did you go to school?"

Ruff remembered the last time Maggie had used that question to bring their exchange under control. He soothed, "We weren't talking sex again."

"You come up with interesting dialogue. You don't fit the trucker's mold too well."

He replied easily, "I own my own truck. I told you my mother is a stickler, just like yours."

"I'm getting hungry."

He hugged her tightly and groaned, "Let's go to my room."

"How could you believe I'd be so crass? I'm talking food? This has been a long day."

He released her slowly and looked at the ceiling as he sighed with a groan, then he smiled at her and took her hand as he walked her along the hallway. "What all did you do today?"

"I still haven't read your letter."

"You can read it anytime. I'll tell you all the things myself. You keep that letter to remind you of me when I'm not around." He smiled at her.

"I'll have to go up to my room. I'll call Phyl and see if she's decent for company. I can't guarantee how the room will look. She isn't especially tidy."

"Debits."

"I'm tidy."

"I remember living with you for several days, and I remember a baby who needed help."

"Don't mention any of it in front of Phyl. No one I know knows anything about us."

He nodded once to acknowledge her comment, but he pulled down his mouth and he raised his eyebrows to indicate his surprise. Ruff explained, "Terry only knows we met at a truck stop."

"That makes me sound like a loose woman."

"He knows you hunt backgrounds for movies. He'd like to be a background for the wicked star who doesn't wear much at all and has all that hair."

"I don't know any of the stars. I never meet them."

"He'll be disappointed."

"If he can get past Phyl, he'll be doing something remarkable."

"I won't tell him that."

"Why not?"

"I've convinced him Phyllis Allen will be a demure lady."

First Maggie gasped in shock, then she laughed at such an impossibility. She told Ruff rather sadly, "We can't leave them alone. He'd be at risk. We have to chaperon them. Curbing her and shielding him."

Ruff commented thoughtfully, "I don't think he's a virgin."

"I didn't know men could be virgins."

"I believe it means anything that's—untried. There're virgin forests."

"I suppose."

"Don't worry about Terry. He's a grown man. He can handle an itchy woman."

"She'll use him up."

Ruff laughed.

"Go ahead and laugh! I just dread having them meet. I will be so embarrassed. She'll probably attack him right off the bat! She'll drag him under the table!"

"No woman you would know would be thataway."

"You mistake the acquaintance. I hardly know her at all. She was vaguely in some of the groups I was with at college. She's still in groups I meet. I have nothing to recommend her. Her parents are in some of the organizations my parents attend. We are not close."

"You're absolved. Terry can handle just about anything." Ruff was placid.

"Good luck to him."

"Let's go eat. I have just the place. It's right here on the ground floor in the complex by the horse statues." He looked at his watch. "We have a half hour to make it. You look great. You needn't change, do you?"

"No. I'll call Phyl to be sure she's ready, then we won't have to sit around, waiting."

She called Phyl from one of the house phones. Then Maggie suggested to Ruff, "Why don't you go over and find the table. Then watch for us? It may be awkward for you to come to the room right now."

Ruff said, "Give me your room number. I don't want to worry about you."

She gave it, and reluctantly left him. It would have been so much different if she'd been there alone, with just Ruff. Phyl was ruining the precious time Maggie had with Ruff. Well, it wasn't entirely ruined, but it was tainted by the intrusion.

As she went to fetch the unwelcome guest, Ruff was calling Terry Benedict.

When Maggie put the card key into the door, it opened and an animated Phyl asked, "Where is he?" in a breathless, predatory manner that hit Maggie all wrong.

Maggie said, "They're waiting downstairs at the table."

"We're eating here at the hotel?"

"Yes."

"Oh." Phyl considered it seriously.

There was no way Maggie was going to allow Phyl to take control and rearrange what was already set. She said, "Come on." And she opened the door.

"Let me check my makeup."

Maggie hurried her. "It's all right. Come on."

"Is this dress okay? You're in a suit."

"You look fine."

"Should I put on a suit? It'd only take a minute."

A tad irritated, Maggie was firm. "No. You're all right that way. Let's go."

Maggie strode through the doorway and off toward the elevator bank with Phyl hurrying to catch up. "I forgot my key."

Maggie stopped. She was not going to be limited to Phyl's comings and goings. She went back and opened their door with her key. "Get it. Come down to the lobby. Go past the horse statues—you can't miss them—to the cashier. We'll be watching for you."

Phyl reached for the key on the table and held it up. "Here's my key."

"Put it in your purse."

"Yes."

Maggie had turned and strode away toward the elevator bank. Phyl ran after her. An elevator was there and they were quick enough to get inside. They went down to the first floor and through the neat and clever baggage area, past the escalator to the second floor and by the two great horses.

The two women did not speak. They got to the cashier area and just beyond was Ruff. He smiled as he caught Maggie's irate eye.

She went to Ruff and said, "We're here," in a way that betrayed her irritation. He took her hand in a comforting manner. He introduced himself to Phyl and smiled. Then he led them through the tables to the five-step stair to another area.

He allowed the two women to precede him up the stairs. That was interesting to Maggie. Phyl was ahead of her.

Beyond, Maggie saw the guy who must be Terry Benedict. He rose from his chair, looking toward them. He was a really neat guy and a total waste to give to Phyl. That barracuda would eat him alive.

Terry was smiling as they approached in a line, weaving between the tables. He grinned at Maggie and said, "You're Maggie. I'm Terry."

They shook hands, and Maggie glanced over to a pale and serious Phyl staring at Terry. Why so pale?

It was probably time for Phyl to have her blood supply from some man's jugular.

With great reluctance, Maggie said, "Phyl, may I present Terry Benedict? Terry, this is Phyllis Allen."

It was done. Maggie washed her hands of the whole shebang. She was not responsible for some innocent Yankee who didn't know better than to accept a blind date.

Terry seated Phyl with ease and sat next to her, asking easy questions and—was that little voice... Phyl's?

Ignoring Ruff's attempt at conversation, Maggie turned her head slowly and stared at her guest. Phyl's eyes were down, her cheeks were pink, her body was tense and rigid.

She was angry? At who all? Not Terry. He was darling. So was Ruff. Only Maggie could be the source for such rigidity. What had she done that had so offended Phyl? How could anyone like Phyl *be* offended?

She looked at the other woman indignantly and with some censure. "Phyl?"

Phyl lifted shy but sparkling eyes to Maggie and grinned widely as she bit her lower lip. She put her hand on Maggie's arm and squeezed it. She was shy? Phyllis Allen? It could *not* be so. It was an act, and she was trying to get Maggie to go along with it.

Maggie gave Phyl a very discreet but hard look of subtle censure and after that, ignored her. But Phyl was very quiet. She laughed at Terry's jokes, but she told none of the outrageous ones Maggie *knew* she knew. Phyl listened to Terry and exclaimed over his stories. She was a full-fledged fraud...one way or the other. Which was it?

It was soon obvious that Terry thought he'd found a real sweet woman, and the shocking thing was that so did Ruff!

When the other two went ahead to choose from the buffet, Ruff chided Maggie, "Phyl is a nice woman."

"Wait for the other shoe."

"Let's see, that expression comes from '—the other shoe to fall'? What will that be?"

"From what I know of her, this is not the real Phyllis."

Ruff considered it. "She's different with women than she is with men? That's not too unusual. Terry is being a gentleman, and his language is undotted with cuss words. So Terry is another Terry right now. Is that what you mean?"

But Maggie squinted her eyes and asked her own question. "Are you different with me?"

"I've never been this way with a woman. Mostly I play pinball machines."

So that gave Maggie something else to think about.

They had each chosen something different to eat, and they took their bread plates and passed around samples to share. They discussed the foods and tasted and compared. It was pleasant and funny. The time whipped past them much too fast. It was as if the precious weekend was being consumed by a greedy Black Hole.

While Ruff shifted on his chair and watched Maggie with possessive eyes, he never once said they should leave and go off on their own. But he wanted to. It was obvious to Maggie that he wanted to.

And her whole, entire body wanted to do that, with him. But she also knew she should not at that time. They would find another time. They would be together. Sometime soon.

She looked at Ruff and remembered how he'd talked and laughed in the tractor cab. How he'd worried about her when the Millstones had intruded. And how he'd held her in his arms, her back against him when the baby slept inside her jacket. And how he'd kissed her so silently while the others slept. But he hadn't taken advantage of her. He hadn't moved his hands on her—as she'd hoped. Wanted.

Ruff was a special man.

Oddly enough, Terry seemed to be similar. He talked and laughed. He teased. He encouraged Phyl's reaction and rejection and sass. He knew what was going on in the world. His speech was like Ruff's. The odd words were clever and not vulgar. Terry hammed speech.

His table manners were acceptable, his manners to a woman were easy and looked automatic. He was another surprise. Ruff had been the first one.

But the shock was Phyllis. She acted like a normal woman. A tad shy, which was a great surprise, then gradually she sassed with some spirit and she laughed. How interesting that Phyl could blush! Who would ever believe that Phyllis Allen could blush about *any-thing!*

Fascinating.

It took them a long time to eat. Then they did the same thing with dessert. They each chose a different one and argued about what the others would choose. Then they passed sample tastes around to the others for critique and comment.

As they were finally leaving, one of the men whose card Maggie had, smiled at her. He said to her, "To-morrow, have lunch with me."

Ruff was the one who replied, "She's mine for the weekend. Sorry."

The man regarded Ruff before he replied, "No, you're not at all sorry."

And Ruff grinned.

They decided to go outside and see if their bodies could walk off some of the food they'd consumed. They were groggy and stuffed. It was April. It was balmy outside. They did walk.

Since Terry was Ruff's friend and knew Ruff loved Maggie, he very adroitly walked ahead and quite cleverly outdistanced the other couple. They went the several blocks over to the Arch and walked along there.

Ruff held Maggie's hand and said, "You're wear-ing my ring."

"Yes."

Ruff glanced at the backs of the preceding couple, and then he leaned to kiss Maggie. He told her softly,

"Our time together will come. Did you bring the circus flashlight?"

"Actually—yes."

He grinned ear to ear.

"You're being very circumspect."

"Does that annoy you?"

She bit her lip to stop her smile. "I'm just impressed."

"I didn't know how you wanted me to act. I could put you down right here on the trampled grass and relieve my pent-up...passion."

"Not here."

The air whooshed out of his lungs, and he stood tall to rub his chest and breathe. He said, "Don't do that to me. You make me look about for a place."

"I'll find one."

He guessed, "The swimming pool?"

"Nobody up there?"

His voice was a bit foggy. "Come to my room."

"When?"

His voice became earnest and his speech was quick. "When is your first meeting in the morning?"

"I don't have to be anywhere until about ten."

"Come to me at eight...seven might not be plausible."

"I know. I'll be with you just before eight."

They walked along, and he swallowed and breathed and his fingers almost hurt hers. "I probably won't get any sleep at all."

"Me, either."

Crossly, he complained, "You're no help at all!"

"Neither are you."

He smiled and swung her hand a little. "So you want me."

"I feel like a cat in heat."

"Now, Maggie, what are you doing to me thisaway?"

"I'm just being honest."

"I love it." He breathed some more. "I'm not sure I'll survive it, but I sure do like to hear you want me."

There were other people around, also walking, so the two couples didn't get too far apart. But the others were obviously guests in the area's hotels and they, too, were out for the air and the walk. It was very pleasant, actually. And for Ruff and Maggie just being together was wonderful. That was a test.

Ruff mentioned, "Apparently Terry and Phyllis are getting along very nicely. She's fooling us with the modest conduct?"

"I've never before seen her with a man, so I don't know how she conducts herself. We are only acquaintances."

"How do you act around other women?"

"It's mostly meetings for some charity or another. With those I roomed with in college, it's like having more sisters."

"What are your sisters like?"

"You know about the one who owns the service stations. And there's one who is a lawyer. And one who is a product rep who calls on doctors. You know about one brother, he's the computer genius, and the other is a coach. He really likes kids. He's a good coach.''

"What's your dad do?"

"He's a lawyer. Criminal law. It can get hairy.''

"How'd you get into hunting backgrounds?''

"A couple of guys I knew in college got interested and coaxed me to do it summers. I like it.''

"Could you be coaxed into another field?''

"I probably could. This job can be lonely.''

"I may make you an offer you can't refuse.''

She put a hand to her forehead and groaned.

9

As they walked along, Ruff said, "When are you going to tell me where you live or how I can get in touch with you, independently?"

"If you should call my house, in two seconds my mother would find out which of your teeth have fillings. She is the wife of a lawyer and—"

"He taught her cross-examination?"

"No. She taught him. She is not a lawyer, but she was born with the talent." Then Maggie made a disgusted mouth and scolded, "Go ahead and laugh. It's true! You should have heard her going at me in those last few weeks."

"What all did you tell her?"

"Nothing! I live at home because I'm so seldom there, but this last time she badgered me shockingly about whom I'd met. About you."

Ruff smiled. "So she knows about me?"

"Not your name. Not yet. She only knows about a trucker taking out my car. I did have to mention that since I didn't take the car home. They looked at me as if I was held together with Scotch tape and glue. They're a terrible burden."

He understood and nodded to show that. "I left home early. I haven't lived at home since I left for college." Then he bit his lower lip. Loose lips sink ships. He'd blabbed.

While Ruff was no billionaire, he had enough to lure a woman who wanted a cushy nest. He wanted a woman who wanted *him*.

She was clever. She watched her steps and allowed the precise pause of casualness to expand before she inquired, "Where did you go?"

He looked at her and even in the lamp-lighted night, the cast of shadows changed their faces. She was being carefully casual. So he knew that she knew his words were a slip, which betrayed the fact that he'd been testing her.

So he was open. "I got a scholarship through my mother's efforts. I told you she's a stickler. She wanted me to go to college, but mostly she wanted me out from underfoot."

"Are you like Phyl and multifaced?"

"Naw. Mom thinks I'm only a nuisance who is too big and noisy. But she does love me. Both parents do, even though I wasn't female."

"I think you use that as a shield against your tenderness for them."

He considered, licking his smile, then he glanced over at her and agreed, "You're right. If we get married, will you promise me we'll have a daughter? Maybe that'd salve their need of a female descendant?"

"Married!"

"Well, it's worth the exploration of ideas together to see if we rub well—otherwise."

"You are salacious."

"Hah! I know what that word means!"

She was not intimidated. "Everybody does—who already knows all the four-letter ones."

His tie loosened, his suit coat open, his hands in his trouser pockets, he narrowed his eyes. "Have you been a school teacher?"

From ahead of them, Terry lifted a hand and asked, "Want to go by the stadium? It's just over that-away."

Ruff asked Maggie, "Okay?"

The stadium was about two blocks from the hotel, so they could walk over to the stadium and then back to the hotel.

She shrugged. "Sure."

Ruff called, "Okay." Then he told Maggie, "We got tickets for tomorrow night's game."

"Good! Four tickets?"

"Yep. We knew we could sell them if anybody didn't show up." Then he reminded her, "I asked if you'd ever taught school."

She lifted her brows. "Preschool."

"Wow! Those teachers are the worst kind!"

She frowned. "Why?"

"They're structured to teach discipline."

She tilted her head back and considered him. "Have you ever been in a preschool classroom?"

He touched his top lip with his tongue before he replied kindly, "Not for some time."

"It's chaos. The primary target isn't discipline. It's trying for quiet."

"So you escaped."

She agreed. "Out into the chaotic world. All the world is sound. Listen."

The under roar of the city was relentless traffic. Cars mostly but also various sizes of trucks and buses, in an endless stream, went past on streets on both sides of the walk, and along the throughway under the crosswalks. There were sirens and horns. There were planes flying past. There were boat blasts. It was all an accepted or ignored muted roar. It was a big city.

Ruff asked, "Would you live in a big city?"

"I do, in San Antonio."

"What do you think of small towns?"

"They are generally quite charming. Everyone knows everyone else and generally they are kin or friends with everyone else." She did not ask him why he'd asked her the question. She assumed it was conversation of the getting acquainted kind. She did ask, "Have you ever lived in a small town?"

"I've only stayed in them occasionally, but mostly I park the truck at a McDonald's. There are other places that have room for truckers. Besides the rest stops, there're burger places and motels that have truck parking areas."

As they crossed another street, she replied, "I've seen those. Once I had the room door open because of the cover smell they adamantly spray in rooms to hide the odors. Whoever selects the smells must have clogged glands in their noses.

"Since I couldn't stand to be inside the room yet, I was in the doorway looking out over the parking lot and the service station next to that. A truck came from the bigger truck parking lot very slowly. He was going so slowly that I was aware the truck was moving wrong. Then I finally noticed the driver was watching me. He was bent down looking across the cab and he waved several times. I wondered if he thought I was, uh, soliciting?"

"So it *was* you! I knew I'd seen you before! No, no. Don't run away." He held her arm, and they had to stop to laugh. He told her, "The truck guys I've run into honestly believe they are irresistible."

"You were." She shrugged and opened out her hands.

He commented in some disgust, "I worked on you for a month of date time and I was wrung out. It took you long enough."

They were by the stadium by then and she retorted, "It was only three days and—"

"I told you it was comparable to twenty-eight days, and by now it's clear into next month!"

The other couple was standing, waiting for them. With some humor, Terry gestured widely and said, "This is the baseball stadium."

Having brothers helps. Maggie looked around and up as she replied, "Oh," as if in surprise, then she added, "I see."

Both men laughed softly in their throats in the way a woman just loves. The humor is so subtle and the liking is there.

But Maggie only looked at Ruff. It was his laughter which she sought. It was his attention she wanted.

They walked back to the hotel, and both couples were holding hands. They didn't release hands as they went into the hotel.

Maggie said to Phyl, "I'll be up in a little while."

Phyl just nodded. Then she turned to Terry and said, "Thank you for such a lovely time. Will you be here tomorrow?"

"I thought we'd go to the museum over at the Arch. Would you?"

"I've never seen it. Maggie?"

And bland faced, Maggie replied, "I have meetings all morning. I'm free for lunch." Only then did she glance casually at Ruff. "How is your schedule."

And he replied quite soberly, "I have a morning meet myself. But I am free for lunch. Let's go to Hannegan's over on The Landing. You guys willing?"

Maggie knew of the place. "We need reservations."

Ruff replied, "I have them. It's a place you'll want to see and the food's great."

They separated from Terry and Phyl, leaving them at the entrance. They walked over to the lounge, which was about deserted by then. They sat a while. And they sighed. And he asked, "All morning?" in a fainting manner.

She slid her eyes over at him and said, "Perhaps it would be wise if you went right up to bed."

"I'll take a couple of aspirin so I don't overreact to the terror facing me in the morning. You said it would be just before eight? Should I eat first?"

Rather elaborately, she looked aside as she considered. Then she solved his problem. "Have breakfast delivered before seven-thirty."

"We'll eat? I hadn't thought we'd have the time."

And she couldn't restrain the laughter any longer.

Having given the other couple enough time, they went discreetly up to her room. They were alone in the elevator and she didn't have any lipstick on by then, anyway, so they took advantage of the situation. No one stopped the elevator. They got to her floor too soon.

Their hands locked, they walked to her door, and he kissed her again.

The door opened and Phyl gasped, "Oh, I thought you forgot your key." And she closed the door.

They barely noticed Phyl. He kissed Maggie again and held her close against his body as he rubbed his hands slowly up and down her back and groaned. He said, "I can last until morning. I have lasted all this time. You are so sweet, Maggie, my heart. I'll see you in the morning. Rest while you have the chance."

She nodded.

He took her card key from her pocket and opened the door, handing the card back to her. She stumbled a little and nodded silently. He smiled.

She whispered, "How can you be that coordinated?"

"I'll help you. Need undressing?"

She opened her mouth for more air.

He told her, "You'd better go on in while you still have the chance."

So Maggie opened the door the rest of the way and turned to look up at Ruff. She just looked at him.

He knew that because he was looking back. He said, "Good night. Sleep soundly."

She nodded. Then her eyelids covered her big eyes, and she slowly stepped back as she closed the door.

She turned to find Phyl standing in her odd pajamas with big sleeves and big legs. Phyl asked, "Did Ruff give you that purple ring?" Then she proved she could be tactful. "It's quite different."

Maggie nodded.

"I've always envied you."

That did catch Maggie's attention and she frowned. "Why?"

"You could always talk to anybody. You were always interested. Guys were always trailing along behind you."

Maggie took her nightgown from a bottom drawer and, speaking logically, she explained, "From nursery school, males bond. When they go away to school, they occasionally go to different schools and they lose their base.

"They're like stray calves. They have no leader. They have no coach. They're lost. Then they discover females are available and without mothers. If you're too kind, they propose... one thing or another. I was only someone who would listen."

Phyl whispered, "Nobody told me that."

Maggie discarded being a guru. "I have older siblings. Times have changed since our parents went away to school. Even now, college is becoming obsolete. The computer rules."

With some surprise, Phyl explained, "I hadn't known you paid that much attention to the world."

That hit Maggie's funny bone and she laughed. She went into the bathroom, closed the door and turned on the shower as she began to undress.

Phyl opened the door, came into the bathroom and sat on the counter. She said, "I need to talk."

"I hope not. I've had a long day and I need to sleep. Save it for lunch."

"I want to know about Terry."

"I have no idea about him other than he appears to be a very nice person." She looked at Phyl seriously. "I wouldn't want you to play with him. He's too nice a guy."

"He scares me."

Maggie stopped midstride in getting into the shower. "How." It was a lead-in word, not a question.

"He's perfect."

"Get to know him better. He could have flaws." Maggie went behind the shower curtain and thought the subject was closed.

She showered with some relish. Her body was very sensitive and that made her think of Ruff. Ruff, that gentle man. She smiled and closed her eyes, glorying in the spray of warm water on her face and down her body.

Eventually, she turned off the water and pulled back the curtain. There on the counter sat Phyl. She'd just been waiting.

Maggie said, "I've not been involved in an all nighter since the first time in junior high school. Having realized through experience that one is exhausted if one stays up all night, I don't. I need to go to bed. I'm sorry if you've a ton of thoughts to exchange. I can't. Hop down and let me brush my teeth. I've got to get to sleep."

Phyl slid off the counter and said a nothing, "Oh." However, she didn't leave the bathroom and go to bed as so obviously expected.

But Maggie had two sisters. She had good friends. She never said one more word. After brushing her teeth, she went into the other room and put her things tidily away. She turned back the coverlet, set the timer for seven and crawled into bed.

Phyl had trailed after Maggie and stood watching before she finally got into her own bed and lay awake.

Maggie strongly resisted even saying another goodnight because that would only uncork Phyl. She turned away, lying on her side, arranged her pillow just right and—remarkably—didn't take very long to go to sleep.

In the morning, Maggie shut off her timer with the first sound. She was rested and exuberant.

From the other bed, Phyl asked, "Can I go to your meeting with you?"

"No. Terry will probably call you if he hasn't already made plans with you." Maggie chose what she'd wear and carried it to the bathroom to dress.

Phyl followed. "I couldn't sleep."

"Sleep now. I'll see you at noon."

Sounding like a lost sheep, Phyl said a nothing, "Yeah."

Putting on enough makeup to appear that she would be in public, Maggie told Phyl, "There's a bookstore downstairs if you're opposed to looking around St. Louis." Then she looked over at Phyl and said, "I thought Terry said you would be going to the museum by the Arch."

"Not until ten."

Maggie went back to her face and looked at herself with some disappointment. She suggested offhandedly, "Then sleep."

Phyl sighed like a lost soul.

Having never been lonely in her life, Maggie's conscience twinged. "There's a Cally Hughes book in my suitcase. Read that."

"I have all her books. I've read them several times."

Being staunch and holding to it, Maggie said, "I'll see you at noon, in the lobby downstairs by the horses."

This time she picked up a purse and made sure she had the card key to the room . . . and the one Ruff had given her for his room . . . before she left, saying, "See you at noon by the horses."

* * *

The rendezvous was easy. No blips, no panics, no upsets. She put his card key into his door and there he was! He was in a bathrobe and rising from a chair as the newspaper dropped from his hands. He took long steps and reached for her.

So they didn't have the covered breakfast right away.

Sometime later, they found the containers were insulated and the food was surprisingly warm still. She was in one of his shirts and her clothes were fortunately the kind she could tie in knots and they still smoothed out instantly. They were scattered around the room in odd places.

She sat in his shirt on a chair by the breakfast cart and looked around. "I do remember coming in the door. What happened to this room? It looks like a tornado hit it. There're clothes everywhere. No. Just my clothes. How strange."

He replied, "Don't go calling attention to yourself."

She took the teacup from her lips and sassed, "I'm probably safe for a while yet."

"Don't push it."

She laughed in closed-mouth delight. Her eyes danced sparkles and she blushed just a bit.

He watched her with the look of an unhungry fox with a mouse. He was interested and he was keeping close track of her. He was wearing underwear shorts.

He hadn't really calmed down. He was being patient with her because she probably needed to eat.

He didn't notice what he ate. He was watching her. She'd gotten her purse and opened it and was hunting inside it.

He was earnest. "I can't believe you're actually here. I wasn't sure I'd ever see you again."

"I knew I'd see you."

He urged. "You have to give me your home address. I won't pry. I promise. If you don't want me to call there or send letters there, get a post office box. I have to have some kind of link with you. Losing you scares me a whole lot."

He gestured. "You could leave the country or get married or just lose interest, and I'd be waiting for the phone to ring. I'd be waiting to hear from you."

"That happens to women. Men dump them."

"You wouldn't be one of those and want to punish just any man, would you?"

"No." She handed him the paper she'd taken from her purse. On it was her parents' names, the address and phone number.

"You trust me?"

"Yes. It's them I'm leery about. They want to know everything. They're like the vice squad—"

"You run drugs?"

"NO!"

And he laughed such a wickedly dirty laugh. He watched her and was amused. But he was especially glad she'd given him her home address.

She tilted up her chin and said, "If you laughed, you must think I'm pure and—"

"You were," he readily agreed, but then he added, "up until I got a hold on you."

"It's true. That shows you're a very bad influence. You've ruined me."

"It was my pleasure."

That old saw. She put a hand to her face and groaned, but her smile was uncalled for.

He suggested, "Come sit on my lap." His hands patted his bare knees.

She gasped in shock. "Your lap is dangerous. There's something nestled in it that is . . . intrusive."

The lights in his eyes danced. But he licked his lips to try to hide his smile as he tried to be earnest. He soothed her. "It's spent. It's harmless. Some woman outwrestled it. It'll be a long while recovering."

"Really?" She put more honey on her already iced breakfast roll. Then she opened her mouth as she closed her eyes and bit into it. She chewed and made appreciating sounds.

He said hoarsely, "Those are the sounds you made in my bed."

That made her forbearingly indignant. "I did not! I lay quietly and submitted with grim courage as you used me."

She ate, prissily aloof, waiting until he got through laughing. Then she swallowed the bite, blotted her lips and said in a perfectly air-brained, dead voice, "You dirty rat."

That only set him off again.

She watched, grinning. Then she told him, "You're easy."

"Yeah."

"No, not that way. I'm talking about your humor. It's easy to make you laugh. No resistance at all."

He agreed. "None."

"You have a one-track mind."

"Come here. Sit on my lap."

"See?" She licked her lips and took another bite from the squishy honey-loaded bun.

"How long can you be here?" His voice was low and serious, but his face was mush. He was vulnerable.

She looked at her watch. "I have a ten o'clock meeting, so we have two hours. Well." She glanced at him as he'd gasped. "Are you okay?"

He crossed his arms in front of himself as he lifted one knee. "I've got to defend my body for another *two hours!*"

She chose some fresh cherries from the bowl and put them on her plate. She comforted him. "Naw. Make it one and a half hours. We can shower together. That'll save time and— You just looked cross-eyed."

"Shower...together? Let's go see if I can handle it."

She stopped and stared at him in a considering way. "You intend to grope me." It was an accusing statement.

He just grinned, watching her.

She considered. Then she said, "Okay. I've never tried that. Let's see if you can stay on your feet."

* * *

It was some time later, and they found they were back in bed again. Her hair was dried enough and she was languid. He was leaning over her, kissing her here—and there—and there.

She said, "Shame on you." But her tone wasn't sincere.

"How'd my tractor know to catch you for me? It just reached out and shoved you off the road. If it hadn't been for the dark blue TEXAS in the middle of your white license plate, I'd have thought you were just a snowdrift." Then he shook his head once. "When I realized you were a car with a person in it, it scared the hell out of me."

"You about scared me to death when you pulled the horn and warned me. You did a marvelous job of adjustment. I hardly felt the crunch. The snow was a great cushion to ease the shock of the impact. Actually, Ruff, you did a remarkable maneuver for us both. You're very skilled."

"When I opened your car door and saw you, I knew my guardian angel had found you for me. It's just a good thing you're not married to anybody else."

She shrugged in a fascinating way that caught his full attention for a while. He had to then move his hands differently.

Eyes closed, she told him, "You're wasting your time."

"Yeah."

She stretched and yawned as she moved her body in the most amazingly subtle ways. He had to just lie there, braced on one elbow, and observe the miracle of it.

She opened her eyes and watched him watch her. She said, "You're really very bold."

He leaned over and scooped her against him. He rubbed his carefully shaven face gently over her cheek to her throat and down to her breasts. He said, "I'm so restrained that my muscles are like rocks."

"I can vouch for this muscle. Oh, it's all relaxed again. How nice. It can rest awhile. Uhhhh, I said it could *rest* awhile. You're very forward. My word! What are you doing?"

"It's just showing off. Ignore it. It's pushy."

He set her laughter off yet again.

Their humor was so softly gentle. So shared. It was the privacy that they treasured. They were alone, together, and no one else could intrude.

He made her blush, he was so curious about her. He smoothed his hands over her and caressed her so sweetly. He kissed her mouth and down her body. He paid no attention to his sex, which was eager yet again.

She asked, "How many women would it take to satisfy you?"

"It's new to this sex stuff. It's been idle and ignored. Now it finds it has a greater role in life and it is a participant. It doesn't realize it's an empty threat by now."

It was so easy to make her laugh.

He told her, "You're so different from me. Look at these." He smoothed his rough hand over her bumpy chest. "I don't have anything that pretty. Look at that.

You're really beautiful.'' He moved his hand down her stomach. "This is such a pretty decoration. Let me see what it covers.''

She gave his hand a token pat and said, "Forget it. You've already been there twice. Don't give me that innocent 'Oh, what's this?' malarkey.''

"You don't think for a minute I'd try to fool you, do you?''

"Yes.''

"You're right!''

How strange that Maggie missed the morning meetings which ended the conference.

Oh, well.

10

Just before noon, Ruff and Maggie showered again.
They were circumspect and that time showered sepa-
rately. They dressed and met Terry and Phyl in the
lobby. The foursome took a cab and went to lunch at
Hannegan's Restaurant and Pub. It was located in the
revitalized nineteenth-century neighborhood close to
the Mississippi.

The area was called Laclede's Landing. The streets
were brick and the street lampposts were cast iron. The
brick sidewalks were lined with small shops. It was a
place for special events.

The Hannegan who started the restaurant was from
St. Louis and was Postmaster General under President Harry Truman. And the restaurant was a replica
of Washington's Senate dining room.

The food was excellent, and the guests talked and
listened to the band. The foursome then walked back
past their hotel. They went on to tour the old court-
house that had been so carefully preserved.

It was a leisurely time.

* * *

The score of the ball game that night was close and the players skilled. The four attendees had popcorn, peanuts and hot dogs. The women had soft drinks and the guys had beer. They were stuffed. They had a good time.

And again, Maggie slept that night in the room with Phyl.

One thing good about couples, it was Terry who took Phyl to the airport. That gave Maggie and Ruff several more hours to go back to bed, hold hands and smile. They never quit touching each other. They were zonked.

He asked her, "Will we get to the point that I can mow the yard while you make me biscuits?"

She looked up into his eyes and guessed, "You're a biscuit man?"

He had his arms around her, and his hands cupped on her bottom. He squeezed her buns as he said, "All kinds." And of course, he used that as an excuse to kiss her yet again.

In his bed, she looked around with some surprise. "Here again! You use every excuse imaginable. When will you run out of triggering?"

"It'll be a challenge for you."

"When you're old and bent and uninterested, I'll have to lure you?"

"We'll see if you can."

But in all that time, he was doing salacious things to

her. He wasn't at all hesitant or modest. He was not the least bit shy.

She made relishing sounds.

It was very tough to face parting even for a while. He coaxed her, "Come along with me. You can read the maps and pour my coffee."

"That sounds exciting."

"We can sleep in the cab."

"That's a strong lure."

He looked smug. "Are you getting susceptible?"

"I wouldn't be at all surprised."

"I have lures I haven't touched, as yet."

"Ohh?"

He nodded in a superior, smug manner. "I have a small black-and-white TV that brings in any local signal around."

"Wow!"

"You're a TV freak! You're so subtle about it that I hadn't known until now. Well, I can figure a way so that you can keep one eye on the screen at all times."

She loved him. Her eyes twinkled and she was conscious of herself, her body and her mouth. She licked her lips and she moved a bit.

He noticed her.

But she was exquisitely aware of him. Her glances were drawn to him, and she touched him. She would slide her smooth hand into his work-roughened one. She brushed against him. She just did it. She wasn't trying to flirt. She just needed to be close to him.

She really wasn't aware of anything about herself. She only saw him, and her hands and glances did the rest of what she wanted. She wanted to look at him. And she wanted to touch him.

He loved it.

Finally, reluctantly, they said goodbye. It was a very tender thing for him, but she was upset. She had never realized their parting could get even tougher. She really didn't want to leave him.

Now, how in the world could she tag along after a trucker? She'd be a nuisance. So she was staunch as she said goodbye. But her eyes held tears and her hands touched him. His arm. His hand. His shoulder. She subtly leaned against his side. Her shoulder touched his arm.

He was excruciatingly aware of her.

They said goodbye several times. They fell silent. They knew they should just go on and get out of there, but neither wanted to go.

Terry came back into the hotel and saw them. Terry signaled Ruff, who watched his friend soberly.

Terry understood the problem and smiled. He waved goodbye with a half salute. And he left.

Maggie didn't notice.

Ruff carried her bag as they took the elevator down to the parking lot below the hotel and went to her car. Ruff put her suitcase in the trunk along with her small bag.

There was nothing left to say. He repeated, "You have the list of where I'll be." It wasn't even a question. He *knew* she had it. He'd had her check her purse twice by then. She did have it, for crying out loud.

And they parted. It took a while. He stopped her as she backed her car from the slot in the underground garage. He leaned over and said through the window, "You have the list?"

With her eyes wide to keep the tears from spilling, she touched her purse.

He said, "Be careful."

For the umpteenth time, she said, "I will."

He drew in a deep breath and looked around before he finally looked back at her. He straightened and patted the car's roof once. Once more he told her, "Take care of yourself."

She couldn't say any more goodbyes. She nodded, yet again.

Finally he stepped back.

She moved the car slowly, slowly away. In the rear-view mirror, he stood in the lane between the ends of the parked cars and he soberly watched after her. She paused at the end of the lane before she turned and looked back at him one more time.

He didn't move. He just stared at her. It was very poignant. She bit her lip and squinched up her face. But the tears did slide down. She took uneven breaths. But she did leave so slowly that he could have caught up with her easily.

Her car crept up the ramp, and her reflexes made her pause, and look, before she drove out onto the street to ease into the traffic.

She drove away, isolated in the crush of cars in St. Louis, Missouri. *Mis-sou-ri?* Misery.

Of course, Maggie did get to read The Letter. She'd gotten that done at a highway rest stop just outside St. Louis. For something she'd once dreaded might be a goodbye letter, she cried seeping tears at the tenderness and attention he'd written to her.

When Maggie finally got to go back home, after another site wrap-up, there was Phyllis, waiting for her.

Maggie unpacked and put things in the washer and dryer while she learned every aspect of Terry's character and conduct, all of which were perfect.

That nudged on Maggie's competitiveness, but if she countered any of the Terry-lecture, Phyllis might never leave. One sure thing, Phyllis was taken with Terry.

After that, while Maggie called Ruff, he wrote her other letters. They were mailed to the P.O. Box at the branch near her parents' home. She bought a padded purple treasure box and kept the letters locked away. When she especially missed him, she opened the box and read the letters. And she felt cherished.

She began to write him notes. They were not elaborate. She did try. She wrote modestly. She felt bold in saying things like, *I love you,* and *You are so sweet,* or *I dream about you even when I'm awake!*

Her stilted notes charmed him for she was a tiger in his bed.

By late summer, they had managed to meet under various circumstances. Once it was in a spring snow at Colorado Springs. Another time their rendezvous was in a wicked wind and dust storm at Rantan, New Mexico. The cab was well sealed. And then they'd met in a heavy rain at Athens, Georgia.

They'd slept in his tractor cab. That was fine for them. They had all the necessities. Each other. But they also had two decks of cards, her Burger King watches—she still had two; he owned the other—his autographed, quarterback Joe Montana baseball cap and the circus flashlight.

They had used that light to find each other in the dark. How ridiculous. Hide-and-seek in a tractor cab? Well, blindfolds helped.

Once when they were lying in his bed, they had shaken the flashlight to make the flickering lights dance magically around his cab. Then some trucker came with his fire extinguisher.

They had to explain and finally show him the flashlight.

Then the intruder wanted one. "I got five kids!"

But Ruff exclaimed, "Five? When was you home enough for that?"

"It ain't that complicated."

The reluctant hosts referred the tenacious intruder to the circus.

He offered them twenty-five dollars!

They chided him for being reckless with his money. They kept the flashlight.

After they parted each time, and counting carefully, he'd ask his love, "Are you okay this month?"

She would reply, "Yes."

At first he was relieved, but as time passed, he began to experience regret.

It really didn't matter where the couple managed to get together. Neither needed to sightsee or visit places of history. Just being together was enough. They made their own history.

They were exuberant just to hold each other. And their murmurings and groans were soft and thrilling. Their touches were hungry, sly and rubbing in greedy exploration.

In their sparse meetings, they really didn't pay much attention to details. Not even food was that important. What it was or how is was served didn't catch their attention. They ate when they were hungry for food.

Then Maggie met Ruff in Childress near the Oklahoma border in the panhandle of TEXAS.

She still wore the purple glass ring. She'd had the band dipped in gold since the original metal had turned her finger green.

The jeweler frowned and lectured her that the base metal was so poor that it wasn't a good foundation for a gold coating. It wouldn't meld. The tacky base would rot.

She was adamant.

The jeweler was disgusted. And he dubiously put better prongs up to hold the purple glass in place.

Since she wore the ring all the time, the soft glass was getting scratched. The sparkle had dulled.

Hers hadn't. She glowed when she talked on the phone to Ruff. And when she saw him, she was blinding to an observer.

He could see no other woman. His eyes and taste had become very narrowed.

Maggie declined Ruff's offer of another ring. He tried to get her to go to jewelry stores and look around. She wasn't interested. She looked at the purple lump gracing her elegant hand and her face was tender.

How could a man cancel that?

So he had begun looking for purple stones that would suit her and replace the glass ring. Tourmalines from South America were available in that color. So were rare star sapphires from India. He was searching for the perfect ring, but it had to be purple.

In the panhandle of TEXAS, she lay in his arms, naked again. She asked him, "How do you know how to write such sweet words?"

And he replied, "On the road, I have a lot of time to think about you and how I feel about you."

She lifted her head and looked down at his moving hand. "You do 'feel' around about on me. I've noticed that."

And she finally got the nerve to examine him minutely and find out how a man's parts work. It was fascinating.

He labeled it as Playing Doctor, and his imagination was exceptional. He insisted on having the circus flashlight on with its sprinkling lights as the bits of colored shadows floated on the ceiling and curtain in the tractor cab.

Licking his lips, his voice husky, his body at attention, he accused her of being a voyeur.

She considered the comment as she was considering him, closely. She replied, "Probably."

She gave him such intimate attention that he thought his brains might blow out. That alarmed him briefly, but his subconscious commented something similar to *What a way to go!*

So he relaxed, but only peripherally, and he began to touch and tease in turn. It was a night that turned them very lax and sighing. And they slept the replete sleep of the gods.

When morning came, and they had to part, she cried. Actually, she just leaked discreet tears, but her lower lip trembled and she sundered him.

Then there was a long dry spell when they didn't see each other. Maggie would call Ruff, and they talked on the phone. She missed seeing him. She wasn't whole without him.

She lost some weight, and she became wonderfully romantic looking. Men watched her with tenderness, knowing they could cure her sadness. She didn't notice them. Even talking to other men, she didn't "see" them.

Women felt compassionate. That was strange because she looked so ethereal and magical that she was a threat of competition. She didn't know that and wouldn't have cared. She thought only of Ruff.

And her mother told her father. "You find out who he is."

Her father asked, "Hmmm?" and he even raised his eyebrows a little, but he didn't take his eyes from the newspaper.

Her mother told her father, "You're the lawyer. You know questioning. You find out." It wasn't quite an admission that she had failed so far.

Her father told her mother, "Okay."

So her father approached Maggie at an inopportune time when she was figuring out her bank balance. He asked, "The man who writes the letters you moon over out in the garden, who is he?"

She didn't even look up. "No one you know."

"Obviously."

"I cannot make this balance. Let's talk another time."

Her dad stood there a while. Then he said, "Give it to me. I'll have the accountant do it."

"No. I shall do this. It's good discipline."

Since that was his out whenever his children wanted to do something, what could her father say?

So he left her alone to wrestle with her checkbook, and he told his wife, who was also Maggie's mother, "She's okay. Just busy."

Not long after that, Maggie was to hunt for a fascinating site in New Mexico and find a chalky, rugged area with scrawny trees and cacti, lizards and snakes and twisted wood. That kind of thing.

So she was driving out through West TEXAS and a truck driver passed her. The space was wide open. There was nothing around but that truck. He pulled his horn and signaled her over.

Yeah. Sure.

He did that a couple of times, driving alongside her and yelling and signaling with his thumb up like they could have a great time together.

She exceeded the speed limit recklessly, knowing that would instantly bring a highway cop.

None came.

The truck came pell-mell and went ahead of her some distance where he stopped his truck. He got out of his cab.

As she went widely around him at some speed, he yelled at her.

The word sounded familiar. He was calling her name? She slowed somewhat and looked back.

He was standing in front of his truck and off the pavement and waving his arms.

He was in trouble? She slowed, watching backward.

He got into his cab.

She stopped, watching back. If he started that truck and moved one inch, she would be out of there.

He came out with a sheet. He laid it on the ground and sprayed something on it. He held it up in front of his truck. It said, *Maggie!*

Hmmmmm.

How did he know her name? Why was he trying to contact her? Was he some yahoo who'd been in the truck stop in Indiana and remembered her? She wasn't driving a red car when she'd been in Indiana. How did he know her? How did he match up another car with her name?

She backed up a little more.

He pointed up.

She stopped and looked. A tornado? She looked back at the trucker. He pointed again.

Away off, she saw a helicopter. Nothing else. A helicopter.

What on earth?

Someone was sick. Her parents needed her? What was the matter?

She backed a little closer but stopped far enough away that if she got out of the car, she was far enough from the danger of a strange man who knew her name, and she could get into her car and drive away.

She got out and stood up.

The trucker hollered, "Maggie!"

She simply stared.

He pointed at the fly in the sky, which was an approaching helicopter. The trucker could still be heard and yelled, "On the CB, he says his name's Rough and

Ready. He's trying to contact you. Do you want me to stick around?''

She grinned and laughed. She jumped exuberantly. She yelled back, "It's *okay!*"

She went around the back of the car and watched the helicopter's approach. She was grinning from ear to ear. Was it really Ruff? How else would the trucker know her name...and his?

The trucker stood and watched.

She told him again, "It's okay! Thank you."

He didn't approach her, but he stood there, watching out for her. A witness. He had a CB.

The chopper landed on the field beyond the fence, causing a turmoil of dust.

Ruff emerged from the silly chopper and stood looking at Maggie, who was at the fence. Then he looked beyond at the careful trucker who was standing close to the head of his truck with his legs spread in a stance of careful observation. With any move, he could be behind the truck, into the cab and calling the highway patrol. He was a good man.

Ruff waved to the trucker, then he leaned inside and shook hands with the helicopter pilot. Ruff took a bag from the chopper and moved away. The chopper lifted and circled as it flew away.

All three watched it go. Then Ruff lifted his bag and walked to the fence. She reached for him.

Witnessing the kiss, the trucker got into his cab, but he didn't move until the pair finished the kiss across the fence. Then he moved slowly, slowly away.

Ruff waved and stood watching after the truck until it was a pinpoint, far beyond.

How many times did she exclaim, "You're here!"

He was full of himself. He pitched his bag over the fence and followed it over in the effortless way of men.

They hugged, there by the fence, for some time. Fortunately, there were no fire ants in that area. An antelope came by and studied them for a while. It lifted its nose and sniffed their scent.

Finally Maggie could ask, "How did you find me?"

"Terry."

"Where's your truck?" Then she sobered, "Did you wreck it?" Her eyes went over him quickly in concern. "Are you all right?"

"I'm on vacation."

And she hugged him to her like the treasure she thought him, and they laughed.

He really was on vacation. So the truck driver drove. They talked. They laughed and they stopped at a deserted rest area, which had been abandoned. There, they made love and they discovered a car isn't as roomy as a tractor cab. He was hanging halfway out of the car, and he mentioned that.

She wasn't deterred.

He said in a growly voice, "You animal."

"It's been too long."

He groaned in agreement, and their lovemaking was elaborate and slow. They relished the being together again in the perfect way of a man and a woman. On the sparsely weeded ground, they finally lay apart, depleted and smiling. They touched each other and, in all that time, only one car drove past. It did not stop. They finally roused enough to tidy themselves. They bathed in the mossy fountain.

The lovers finally settled into her red car, and they went on their way, but they went quite leisurely.

They felt they had time, and that was unusual. They had time. They were together for longer than just a weekend.

She asked, "Will you bore me after you finally sate me?"

"Probably. I haven't much chatter that I can use to a woman. My communication is almost entirely on the CB. Men tend to have a different view of life and love."

She questioned, "Why?"

"We're a different race."

She could agree with that. "Obviously."

"We're not only physically different, our thinking is different."

She even said the words, "I'll agree to that. How did you find the helicopter?"

"I rented it and the pilot."

Then she tilted her head as she looked at him down her cheeks. "How'd you know how to find me?"

"Terry told me how to find Phyllis. She told."

A trifle disgruntled, she made the sound, "Ah."

"She has no clue how private and withholding you are."

"How can you, of all people, say that I'm withholding?"

He loved it.

"So Terry contacted my parents?"

"No. Phyl did. I said I didn't have enough quarters to explain myself to them, and she could just ask. I called her back."

"Phyllis." Of all people to be involved with her and Ruff, it had to be ... Phyllis.

"She didn't ask any questions. She was very nice."

And so was Ruff. Maggie looked over at him, driving her car down a strange highway and seeming very familiar with the area ... She asked, "Have you been out here before?"

"Yeah."

"When?"

He looked over at her. "Several times. I do know all the best places to park and eat."

"You would know that."

So they drove off into the sunset, to adventure, to contentment. It was an interesting time.

Meanwhile, the crew at her headquarters was wrestling over a title for last winter's shoot in Indiana. Linda was there, Josh and Jon were also. There was a scattering of others.

Somebody remembered Maggie and a truck driver were caught in the snowstorm.

"I hear they've seen each other since then."

"Is that right?"

Linda said, "Yeah. He really was sweet to Maggie."

Jon mentioned, "It took that storm to get them together."

Josh was practical, "But without the storm, we wouldn't have found the background for *Smalltown*."

One of the gathering groused, "That's a thirties title. We have to find something else."

Jon reminded them, "The big boys like it."

Josh mused with narrowed eyes, "Let's try for something else."

That was how it came about that *Smalltown, Indiana*, became the blockbuster film titled *Not Looking For a Texas Man*.

* * * * *

SPECIAL EDITION

Stories of love and life, these powerful novels are tales that you can identify with—romances with "something special" added in!

Fall in love with the stories of authors such as **Nora Roberts, Diana Palmer, Ginna Gray** and many more of your special favorites—as well as wonderful new voices!

Special Edition brings you entertainment for the heart!

SSE-GEN

SILHOUETTE® *Desire®*

Do you want...

Dangerously handsome heroes

Evocative, everlasting love stories

Sizzling and tantalizing sensuality

Incredibly sexy miniseries like **MAN OF THE MONTH**

Red-hot romance

Enticing entertainment that can't be beat!

You'll find all of this, and much *more* each and every month in **SILHOUETTE DESIRE**. Don't miss these unforgettable love stories by some of romance's hottest authors. Silhouette Desire—where your fantasies will always come true....

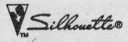